Justice
and
Revenge

Holly Fox Vellekoop

Other books by Holly Fox Vellekoop, MSN

STONE HAVEN: Murder Along The River (Avalon)

How To Help When Parents Grieve: Practical Methods to Help Grieving Parents (Blue Note Books, Florida)

www.hollyfoxvellekoop.com

ISBN-10:0615574378
ISBN-13:978-0615574370

DEDICATION

This book is dedicated to those who have supported this novel:

My husband Ronald B. Vellekoop who is my favorite editor and responsible critic.

Authors Valerie Allen, Lee and Vista Boyland and Marshall Frank for reviewing the unedited manuscript, making constructive comments, and suggestions.

Author and editor Mia Crews for her hard work and assistance in gaining publication of this novel.

My six fabulous grandchildren just for being you: Josh Seidel, Rachel Seidel, Zachary Seidel and Levi Seidel; Elijah Seidel and Cally Seidel.

To the law enforcement officials, dog handlers and others who contributed their expertise for their prospective input.

And to those for whom justice has been denied.

PROLOGUE

Shivering with fright, the young boy clung to his mother. She wrapped a blanket around him and softly sung a tune to calm her only child.

His anxious father rubbed the boy's back, gently repeating his name. "Vincent, Vincent . . ."

Between efforts at comforting his wife and son, phone instructions were given to Security. A flurry of calls made and received consisted of few words, but plans were in the making.

"I want you to make them pay for this," the boy's mother said through tears. "He could have been killed."

The father lifted his wife's chin with his hand. "I vow to you with everything we have, they will be sorry they held him for ransom. They won't get away with it, I swear." He called long-time acquaintances across the globe with expertise in such things.

"We'll gather tomorrow with our ideas," some offered.

"This may take time, expense and a dedicated group," the father said. "But we *will* get them."

CHAPTER ONE

Cold water from the outdoor shower-head felt refreshing on her hot body. Lissa turned herself about, cleaning the lotion, ocean salt and sand from head to toe, being careful not to dislodge the colored contact lenses from her eyes. She maneuvered her bikini, pulling each piece out from its edges, to allow the water to cleanse the skin covered by the green material. Water coursed over a tiny Atala butterfly tattoo on her supra-pubic region, unseen with this particular swimsuit. She kicked off her sandals and washed them. Bending down and exposing cleavage, she placed the sandals on her feet. Lissa turned her legs about, flexing calf and thigh muscles to show off long beautiful legs. Mindful of admiring gazes nearby, she prolonged the process.

"Hey redhead," one of the young men hollered to her. His eyes sparkled with interest.

"Hey, yourself," Lissa said back.

"What's your name?" he said.

"What's yours?"

"I asked first," he replied.

"So you did." She smiled her best and continued showering.

The line lengthened, so Lissa turned off the water and another young woman took her place. She pulled a colorful beach towel from her bag and walked toward some trees by the bathhouse. She briskly dried her body, subtly enhancing her physical attributes with movement. When she finished, she rubbed her long, red hair, wrapped the towel around her waist and got a hairbrush out of her bag.

Several groups of two or three young men, and a few solitary ones, pretended they were there just for a discussion, not wanting to get caught staring at the bathing girls. But they were watching nonetheless. There was the occasional whisper when a particularly pretty girl in a skimpy bikini would take her turn under the water. When two girls got beneath the shower-head at the same time, it brought the full attention of the boys their way.

One older man was frowning as he watched the males watching the girls, including his granddaughter who was using one of the showers. When his granddaughter rinsed the sand from her body, the old man stood between her and the boys, blocking their view a bit. Occasionally, he would glare at them and mutter.

"Hey, we're not hurting anyone," one of the young men said.

"Move on," the grandfather replied. When he saw them lingering, he said, "Now."

A few of the younger boys went to the beach but the rest stayed put.

The elderly man ushered his granddaughter further down the boardwalk.

Lissa was aware of the groups of boys that leaned against the boardwalk railing, watching the females taking turns using the cold spray of water to wash away hours of lying in the sand. The males' ages varied from early teens to early twenties. It was a pleasurable spectator sport for them. Today, Lissa was their favorite.

One of the watchers had caught Lissa's attention, too. A young man the other boys called Craig. She liked that he was looking at her and noticed he pretended to be embarrassed by it. He appeared to be a teenager of about eighteen years of age. Like most of the young men around him, he was slim, with a hairless chest, his skin brown from the many hours spent at the ocean's edge. He had medium-length hair sticking out from under a "Gators" baseball cap. His bright yellow surfboard rested behind him against the outside of the railing while he took a break from hitting the waves to do some girl watching.

Lissa was impressed. From what she had learned about him prior to this morning, he was everything she thought he would be and more...youthful-looking with a handsome maturity, self-assured and direct. *You sure look full of yourself, and you definitely have the bearing of a teenager. But we know who you really are.*

Craig Bergen was not looking at the other girls. Instead, he kept his eyes on the redhead. He had seen her around and was sure she was interested in him. He felt an instant attraction. He especially liked her long, shiny red hair and fair skin. She was slim and leggy, in her late teens, and he thought her to be perfect. Just what he was looking for.

Lissa picked up her plastic beach bag, stuffed the damp towel deep inside and readied herself to leave. She passed the staring males and padded on the boardwalk toward her job at the surf shop. Glancing to her left at the one who called himself Craig Bergen, she smiled broadly, wanting to send a signal she was interested.

He repulsed her, but Lissa was adhering to the Script her group had written. She was baiting the hook.

The other males appeared disappointed she hadn't looked their way.

As she passed, Craig tried to see if she had green eyes. He smiled broadly when emerald gems looked seductively back at him. For him, this was just another easy conquest in the making.

"She's a hot one," she heard one of the boys say.

"She's a freakin' doll," another one said.

"Cool it," Craig said in a voice loud enough for Lissa to hear. "She's a nice girl."

Lissa's opinion of Craig's performance jumped a couple notches when she heard him chide them. Her cell phone rang a tune, and she answered it. "I'm sure he'll be here again tomorrow. Maybe I'll get lucky and he'll ask me out. If not, I'll make the first move."

CHAPTER TWO

"Maybe your little girl would like this color," Lissa said brightly, holding up a hot pink swimsuit for the mother to see. "It would be a good shade for her, with her hair and skin color."

Working in the surf shop provided contact with children which Lissa enjoyed. The work wasn't difficult, and she had a talent for it.

"I love it," the youngster said to her mother. "I want it. And these other swimsuits, too. I want them." The mother agreed and purchased what her pampered daughter asked for.

"I've been watching you the weeks you've worked for us, Lissa. You have quite a way with the customers," Albert said to her.

"Thank you, sir," Lissa said. "I really don't do anything special. I'm respectful of them and try to find items I think they would like." She shrugged her shoulders and smiled.

"You don't realize it, but there's more to it than that," Albert said. "Customers appreciate it when a salesperson goes the extra mile for them. You're polite, you find the things they like, and you hold the items for them, replacing them on the hanger when they're done, and do just about anything they ask - all with a smile. I haven't found too many teenagers who know how to do that. You're very mature for a seventeen-year-old."

"I just treat them the way I like to be treated," Lissa said. Uncomfortable with speaking about herself and feeling a little nervous the way the conversation was going, she rearranged some stock on the counter. A mental note was made to ramp up her behaviors to appear more like a teen.

"That says it all, right there," Albert said. "Even though you've not worked here long, I want to reward you for your hard work. I spoke with the store's owner and told him how our sales have increased since you started this job. He agrees with me that you'll be getting a raise in your paycheck next week."

"Thank you, sir," Lissa said. "I appreciate it. I can use the extra money for school clothes and books. Classes will be starting soon, and I'll need to be ready."

"Just keep up the good work," Albert said. "Speaking of which, I think you have another customer." He nodded his head in the direction of a young male who had entered the store.

The customer was taking expensive designer eyewear from a rack and looking at them. He fidgeted with each pair, trying them on.

"Of course," Lissa said. "Thank you, again."

She went to see if he could use some help and recognized who it was.

"Hi," the young man said.

"Hi," Lissa said, her heart beating a little faster. *Things are looking up. He's nibbling the bait.*

"My name is Craig Bergen. I saw you at the beach today. Remember?" He smiled broadly and removed his sunglasses so she could see his eyes.

"Yes, I do," Lissa said. *He's even cuter up close. No wonder he's so good at what he does. His looks pave the way for his actions.*

"What's your name?" he asked. He glanced at himself in the mirror, saw something on his face near his mouth, and wiped it off.

"Ice cream," Bergen said with a self-conscious grin.

"I love ice cream, too," Lissa said, laughing. "Strawberry's my favorite."

"What's your name?" he asked again.

"Lissa. I work here in the afternoons. I usually go to the beach in the morning at the same place where I saw you, then I come here to work."

"Maybe I'll see you there tomorrow morning."

"I'll be there."

"I'll look for you. Maybe we could talk or something."

"Sure. Remember, I can only stay until noon because I have to work."

"I'll keep that in mind," he said, studying her face. "You from town?"

"All my life. I love this area. All my family and friends are here."

"Great," he said.

Bergen put his sunglasses on and carried two other pairs plus three beach towels to the checkout counter. He paid with cash and turned and smiled at Lissa. Just as quickly as he had arrived, he was gone.

"Who's that guy?" Albert asked.

"He's a young man I met at the beach this morning," Lissa said. "His name's Craig Bergen. He seems like a nice guy. He wants to see me at the beach again tomorrow morning." She beamed.

"Do you know anything about him?" Albert asked. "You have to be careful, you know. But I guess your parents talked to you about all that. I worry about girls going out with guys they don't really know. It can be dangerous."

Even though it was the first time he had met him, something about the teenage boy didn't sit right with Albert. It was nothing tangible, just a father's instinct.

"Don't worry. I'm very careful," Lissa said. "I'll ask around about him before I get involved. Just to make sure he's what he says he is. And my parents will want to meet him before we date." She flashed a big grin. "They're big on knowing who I'm with and where I am." She rolled her eyes as if to indicate it was a nuisance.

Albert was relieved to know that. Young women up and down the east coast had been put on alert since a killer the press called 'The Beach Boy' was wanted for the murder or disappearance of teenage girls and suspected in the rapes of others.

Lissa stopped talking and absently rubbed her fingertips together lightly. She peered closely at the reddened areas and pulled some skin away.

"Something wrong?" Albert asked. "Your fingers hurt?" He reached for her hands, but she put them behind her.

"No. No. Nothing. I think I've developed a bit of an allergy, that's all." She rubbed them behind her back and said, "Here's another customer. I'm off to make some sales."

Holly Fox Vellekoop

CHAPTER THREE

It was early morning and the sun was shining brightly across the sands and out onto the white-capped turquoise water. Tourists and locals were parking their vehicles, opening trunks and removing swim supplies for a fun day in the sand and the waves. As usual, Florida weather was cooperating.

A dark car pulled up to the sidewalk at the intersection near the beach parking lot, and Lissa, wearing a green bikini with a white cotton over-blouse got out. She put her beach bag across her shoulder and, waving goodbye to the driver, headed for the walkway leading to the beach.

"Have a safe day," the driver called to her, before pulling out into the traffic. He watched her in the rearview mirror for as long as he could.

"You, too," she yelled back to him. She put in some numbers on her cell phone and spoke. "Hello, Daddy?"

"Hi, Lissa," a male voice said. "Where are you?"

"I'm on the boardwalk, heading for the beach. You know my plans for here, all according to the Script. After that, I'm going to work for the afternoon. I'll call you from there."

"Everything okay?" Daddy asked. He wanted to make sure his favorite caller was safe. This Play was important, but the lives of his Players trumped everything, especially Lissa. Daddy permitted himself moments of reminiscing of his immediate strong attraction to her. She was everything to him, regardless that their love broke his rule of 'No relationships between or amongst Theater Group members.' She's worth it, Daddy rationalized, and permitted the girl of his dreams, kind and sweet, comforting and strong, to occupy his immediate thoughts and emotions.

"Yep. Talk to you later. Love you."

"I love you, too."

Lissa walked toward the water where waves were pounding against the shore. The surf was especially high today with a strong tide. Colored flags were flying, warning of a strong undertow. She determined not to go too far out.

Lissa spread a blanket just a few feet from the water. She placed her beach bag down and peered inside to make sure the 22 caliber handgun was safely wrapped up at the bottom. She sat down and got comfortable, feeling more secure because of having the weapon. With her knowledge of 'The Beach Boy,' she wasn't taking any chances.

Lissa's parents approved of the hidden firearm ever since Lissa's sister, Kelly, was attacked in her freshman year at college.

She shuddered at the thought of her lovely sister's body, muscles wasting and hands and feet contracting from immobility. Kelly's promising future was stolen by her attacker Rick Cline. The same Rick Cline who now calls himself Craig Bergen and is known as 'The Beach Boy' to law officers.

Lissa felt saddened about the suffering her older sister had endured during her rape and beating, being left for dead. She reminisced about when the police picked Cline up, they had also confiscated his computer and hundreds of photographs he had bought and sold on the Internet. Some were pictures of foreign women supposedly looking for American husbands. There were also computer files of bondage web sites with images of women being sexually dominated in vulgar, perverted poses by men of all ages and enough pornographic materials to fill boxes.

After progressing through the court system, like many others across the country, Kelly received no justice to which she was due. Her sister promised to do what she could to change that and was working on it now.

Lissa pushed those images from her mind to concentrate on the plan for the morning. She smoothed her red hair, pulled back in a ponytail trailing down around her neck. Not wanting to suffer a sunburn, she lathered herself all over with sunscreen and adjusted her bikini, the color which highlighted her eyes.

The sun beat down on the loose sand, reflecting shells and sargassum weed. Lissa resisted the urge to get up and poke around amongst the drying wrack for sea beans, by-the-wind sailors, sea hearts, and other lovely treasures that drift lazily across the seas, all of which get tangled in the floating plants as they follow the Gulf Stream or Yucatan current and wash up on the shores to be found.

She looked around to see who was at the ocean this morning. There were forty or fifty people at the beach, but she was looking for one person in particular. She squinted across the small crowd for her target, ready to get the scheduled Play started.

Down near the water's edge, an elderly couple sat on chairs in the brine, chatting while splashing their feet in the ocean waters. The husband leaned over and said something into his wife's ear which caused her to nudge him playfully and laugh.

Parents with small children watched their little ones toddle toward the water where they splashed and giggled. Bigger offspring made sand castles to show to anyone who would stop and remark on them. They used their hands and shovels to dig deep to expose tiny creatures, dug them out, and squealed with delight as they rushed to show them to their parents.

Young men and women with surfboards tethered to their legs were out on the waves. It was a typical gathering for this time of day and month of the year of families and friends enjoying the inviting Atlantic Ocean at Indialantic, Florida.

"Lissa," a young man's voice said from behind. A shadow fell across her blanket when he stepped closer.

Lissa shivered then recovered.

Bergen smiled, his gaze revealing admiration.

He placed his beach blanket next to hers after she invited him to sit next to her. He sat down and clasped his arms about his legs, looking out at the ocean through his newly purchased sunglasses. His yellow surfboard was stuck in the sand behind them.

"It's beautiful here. Sunny and warm. And the ocean is much nicer than up north," he said.

"Then you're not from Florida?"

"No, I'm from here," Craig lied. "But I've visited family in Atlantic City, New Jersey. And I vacationed at the ocean in

Maryland, and Delaware, too. Right now, we live in that motel there," he said, gesturing to an older three-story yellow building behind them. A large neon sign advertised the building as The Banana Motel, a local landmark for its name and color.

"You are so lucky to live right on the beach," Lissa said. "I have to drive twenty minutes and then cross the causeway to get here. I live on the mainland."

"It's only a temporary arrangement," Bergen said. "Our house is being remodeled top to bottom. The contractors won't be done for months. I'm really getting tired of living in a motel." He broke from the conversation and looked out to the Atlantic, smiling his best in an attempt to get her to like him.

"I'm sorry to hear you're out of your home. But, the good thing is that it's time limited. It will be worth it when you finally get back in." She studied his face. "Not to change the subject, but how old are you and are you still in school?"

"I'm eighteen. I just graduated this year. From one of the charter schools. I'll be starting at Auburn University in Alabama in the fall. How about you?"

"I'll be a senior this year at a parochial school. I'm seventeen," she said. "I'll be soooooo glad to graduate."

Throughout the morning, the two shared stories of their lives with the nonstop dialogue that new acquaintances do. They ran in and out of the water, swimming near the shore to avoid being carried out to sea by the strong undertow. Other times, they floated, holding onto each other, enjoying the water and flirting.

When they were back on their blankets, Lissa's cell phone rang a couple times, and she carried a short conversation before hanging up.

"I don't have a cell phone," Bergen said. "Can't afford it."

"My parents insist I have one so they can keep in touch with me. They're always saying, 'You can never be too careful.' "

"Very true. There're some weird characters in the world." He beamed confidently as if he were not one of those she should be worried about.

"I'll have to be leaving soon," Lissa said. "Work." She rolled her eyes as if the thought was disagreeable and started to gather her belongings.

"Do you think we could meet somewhere tonight? Just to go for a walk or something?" He helped her pick up some of her items.

"Sure," Lissa said. "Where?"

"How about right here? This is close to where we're staying, and hardly anyone comes here at night. What's a good time for you?"

"Is 8:30 a good time? I'll be off work by then and will have had dinner with my family. And my homework will be finished. Will that work for you?"

"That would be great. We'll be finished with dinner then, too." The late hour would insure they had the cover of darkness which pleased him.

Bergen helped Lissa gather her things together, careful not to stare at her bikini-clad figure.

She placed the items down and gave him a brief hug. His body was warm, and he smelled like coconut suntan lotion.

Lissa noted how smooth his skin felt and, though it repulsed her, gave a little squeeze of encouragement before letting go.

After hugging her, he gathered his own belongings. So far, his experiences with the pretty girls confirmed his conclusion that they are all pretty stupid about boys and life.

"I bring so much junk when I come here," she said, picking everything back up. She pushed her towel down into the beach bag, covering the items beneath.

"Here, I'll carry that for you," Bergen said, reaching for the bag.

Lissa kept a firm grip on the bag which held her firearm. "No, that's all right, you carry this." She handed him her blanket which he shook out and folded.

He resisted pulling her close for another hug, not wanting to be too forward yet. If all went according to plan, there would be plenty of time for that later.

They walked together across hot sand to the boardwalk which led to the parking lot.

Lissa pulled her phone out, punched some numbers and said, "Hi Daddy. I'm on my way to work, now." She listened for some short instructions and hung up.

"Parents," she lied to Bergen. "They always want to know where I am."

"Mine, too. But that's good. Keeps you safe," he said. "I'm looking forward to seeing you tonight." He flashed his killer grin. "And maybe I'll get to meet your parents sometime."

"Sure. They'll want to meet you if we are going to date. I don't think I'll tell them about tonight, though. I'll just say I'm going somewhere with my girlfriends. First dates can be awkward."

"Yeah, that's for sure. See you at 8:30." He was thrilled, convinced again by her response to him, that he was right - the pretty girls are stupid. This girl was willing to meet him alone and not tell anyone whom she was meeting.

"Oh, if I'm late, don't worry. Just wait for me, okay? I have homework to do." She smiled coyly, cocking her head to the side.

Bergen waved to her as she crossed A1A at the traffic light to work.

Lissa waved back and yelled, "Remember to wait for me. Okay?"

Bergen was pleased that they would be meeting at the beach. It would be dark, and there would be no lights shining there because the turtles were nesting. He was mindful of the ordinance against any businesses casting light on or near the beach. Without the artificial light to distract them, the newly hatched turtles would drag themselves toward the moonlight dancing on the ocean and freedom, instead of crawling to the lighted highway and certain death. He was excited that the darkness would give him the necessary cover but thought it stupid for anyone to care about a bunch of turtles.

Lissa changed her clothes in the bathroom at the surf shop. She ran a brush through her hair, looking at herself in the mirror to make sure her makeup was still good. She placed her cosmetics and beach bag in her locker and prepared to work. She deliberately fingered the locker door for just a moment, transferring her prints to the metal. She considered her job and how much she enjoyed selling beach items to the customers. She was going to miss the friends she had made already.

"Hi," Lissa said to her supervisor. "How's business today?" She smiled and immediately began her shift, straightening up clothing that customers had carelessly re-hung on the racks or tossed somewhere.

"Business is slow, but it will be better now that you're here," Albert said. "Looks like you were at the beach again this morning."

"Yep. It's the best way to begin the day." She laughed. "As I always say, we sea turtles have to be near the water."

"I used to be that way, too, when I was your age. I'm a Florida native. Wouldn't want to be anywhere else." He looked at his young salesgirl. "Where are you originally from? I detect some kind of an accent but can't seem to pin it down. If my wife were to hear you, she'd pinpoint it. She's very good at that."

Lissa's pulse jumped a bit and wanting to change the subject, she blurted, "Oh. Guess what. Remember that teenager who was in the store here yesterday? Craig Bergen. Real cute. Bought some sunglasses and stuff."

"Tried on all the sunglasses and bought two pairs and three towels," Albert said, all proud of himself for his memory. "Sure, I remember him. Why?"

"We're going out tonight. Meeting at the beach at 8:30," Lissa said, making sure he heard her every word.

"Good for you. Not to take away from your excitement, but have you found out anything about him? I wouldn't want a nice girl like you getting involved with someone who could be trouble."

"Yes, I have. We met again this morning at the beach, and he told me all about himself. He's eighteen-years-old. Graduated from a local charter school. Will be going to Auburn University in the fall. Loves to surf. Lives at a motel with his parents. Likes rock and roll. Doesn't drink alcoholic beverages. And he has family in New Jersey." She kept working.

"Wow. You found out a lot about him. What do your parents think? I want to know what my daughters are doing and who they're going out with, so I'm sure your parents do, too."

"They said it's all right as long as I keep my cell phone nearby and call them frequently. So, that's my plan."

"What's he doing living in a motel?" Albert asked. "That's a bit unusual."

"He said his home is being remodeled and taking longer than they thought it would. Guess the construction crew had lots to do."

Albert screwed up his face at that explanation. "Hmmm. That's possible."

The front door opened and a young couple entered the store.

"Gotta get to work," Lissa said. "Talk to you later."

CHAPTER FOUR

Eight-twenty pm...

A dark car pulled up at the corner of A1A and Fifth Avenue in Indialantic. The back door opened and Lissa emerged. She adjusted her white, short-sleeved, cotton blouse down over a white, flowing cotton skirt. Her clothes reflected what little light was available, making her visible to anyone watching. On her feet, she wore gray ballerina slippers with beads on top and laces that tied around her lower legs almost up to her knees. She tapped her left side to be sure her cell phone was still there and was comforted in feeling the hard case.

"Be safe," the driver said.

"Thanks," Lisa said. "Tell Daddy I'm going to meet Bergen now. This Act of our Play is ready to begin."

"Will do. See you real soon," Benny said. He gave a short wave as he inched back into the slow moving traffic heading north along the ocean.

"I'm on my way. I just dropped her off at the beach and will swing around to pick her back up," Benny said into his cell phone. "She said to tell you she's on her way to meet him. One thing, Daddy. I'm not sure, but I think I'm being followed."

"Lose them," Daddy said. "And double around, change cars and follow them. Then get back to me when you find out who they are."

"I'll do my best. If they're able to follow me, they're pretty good. But I'm better." He sped up, skillfully moving in and out of traffic before making a U-turn.

Lissa trembled as she thought of tonight's Act. Her skin felt clammy despite the warm evening. It was always this way when she was doing a Play and setting someone up. It was exciting, but scary. A black, lightweight, long coat was folded and carried underneath her left arm. She tucked it in tighter, making it barely noticeable.

"Yoo hoo. Lissa," a woman's voice called out to her from a beach house near the boardwalk. "Yoo hoo. Look, Helen, it's Lissa," the older woman said to her friend. She waved her arms to get the girl's attention. "Come over and say hello. We want to see you."

Lissa walked over to the dimly lit patio where the voice was coming from. "Hi, Mrs. Anderson. How are you?" She gave the older woman a hug.

"I'm good, dear. And I've told you repeatedly to call me Ginny," the kindly woman said, tsking and grasping Lissa's hand. She pointed to a friend sitting at the table with her and said, "This is my neighbor, Helen. You remember Helen, don't you?" She pulled Lissa closer so her friend could get a good look.

Helen, a senior citizen like Ginny, smiled and greeted Lissa.

"Ginny invited me to dinner tonight. Wasn't that nice?" Helen said. "We made plans weeks ago to eat dinner here on the patio and enjoy the lovely evening." She looked closer at the girl. "I remember you from somewhere."

"It was nice of her to invite you. And I remember you, Helen. You came with Ginny a couple of times into the surf shop where I work. Nice to see you again." She shook Helen's offered hand. Plans were working out well. Both ladies would definitely remember her being here.

"That's where I know you from. Of course. What are you doing out tonight?" Helen asked. "And looking so pretty."

Ginny smiled knowingly. "You do look lovely, Lissa."

"I probably shouldn't be telling you, but I'm meeting a date here at the beach. His name is Craig." Lissa smiled. "Craig Bergen. It's our first date."

"Do we know him, Ginny?" Helen asked. "Craig Bergen," she repeated. "Hmmm. No, it doesn't ring a bell. What's he look like?"

"He's that cute young man we see around here once in awhile," Ginny said. "Yellow surfboard. Lives at The Banana Motel over there." She gestured toward a yellow building up the beach from her home. "Always carrying that surfboard around."

"I know who you mean now," Helen chirped. "He's good-looking, Lissa. How old is he? I can never tell anybody's age anymore, they all look so young. It used to be a lot easier."

"He told me he is18," Lissa said. "One year older than me. I gotta get going now or I'll be late for my date."

"Look how pretty you are in that beautiful outfit. He's gonna be dazzled," Ginny said. "And look at those cute little shoes." She and Helen admired the way the gray ballerina slippers were shining in the patio light.

Lissa, mindful of how important it will be for the women to remember what she was wearing, pulled her skirt up a little so they could get a closer look at her shoes.

"Now get going," Ginny said. "So you don't disappoint your young man." She had a mischievous grin. "I never bought into that 'keep them waiting' thing that some girls did. I was always on time for my dates." She looked smug. "And I had plenty of them, in my day."

"You two have fun tonight," Lissa said as she walked away. "Enjoy yourselves. I'm glad I got to see you."

The women waved as the young woman walked toward the boardwalk and down the steps leading to the beach.

"Remember what it was like when we were that age, Ginny?" Helen said. "Oh my goodness. To be young like that again. Reminds me of my husband Alvin. In our day, we'd get dressed up pretty, too, and go to meet our sweethearts."

Ginny nodded. "I remember everything as if it was yesterday," she said, as she thought of the small figure gliding toward her rendezvous.

Her thoughts were different from Helen's. They were focused on the birth of her only child, Bobby. His chubby little face and sweet disposition. She reminisced of him growing into a toddler, a child, teenager, young man, a good, responsible, community-minded citizen. He had been a good son, and suddenly he was murdered. Her heart ached as she thought of the justice which will be served for Bobby with the Theater Group's play.

Helen asked Ginny about the dessert they were eating, bringing her back to the present. The women resumed their visit with Ginny reminding Helen of the outfit Lissa had been wearing. They discussed her lovely shoes in detail.

Treading lightly on the wooden stairway, Lissa stopped before getting all the way down the steps. She pulled the long, black coat out from under her arm, put it on, and buttoned it up, covering her white outfit completely. She pulled the hood up over her hair and walked briskly along the sea-grape brush, away from where Bergen was waiting. She called Daddy on the phone and scheduled the driver to pick her up.

Down at the beach...

Bergen was walking at the ocean's edge, eagerly awaiting his target. Hands in his pockets, he fumbled with items there, wanting to be sure everything was ready. He looked out over the dark waters, rolling in and out of the shore, keeping an ancient beat. It mesmerized him for a moment, but he resumed his focus on Lissa's arrival and his plans for her.

He pulled a small light from his key-chain and shined it on his watch. Eight-forty-five. Alone in the dark, he was concerned. Then he remembered how Lissa had told him she might be late and he was to wait for her. Those were her last words, so he assumed something must be holding her up.

He walked back and forth on the firmer sands at the water's edge. He didn't mind the wait. Extensive preparations had been made for this evening. Back at his motel room, everything was in its place. He loved it when his plans worked out so well. He was ready to add another name to his list and the photographs he planned on taking to help him relive the event.

CHAPTER FIVE

The next afternoon...

The two elderly women were greeted warmly by Albert as they entered the surf shop. Ginny went in first, holding the door for her slower friend, then turned to the clerk. "How are you, dear?" Ginny asked. "You know my friend, Helen," she said, nodding at her companion.

Helen greeted Albert.

"I'm fine," Albert said. "And yes, I remember Helen. You came in here before with Ginny. Bought sunscreen both times. Can I help you with anything today?"

"What a memory you have," Helen said. "Do you know that much about all your customers?"

"I know my customers," Albert said. All they have to do is come in here once, and I've got them up here." He tapped his temple. "And I've known Ginny for many years. We're old friends." He smiled her way. "She used to work for me here at the shop."

"And I enjoyed every minute of it, Albert. But, today I'm looking for a new sunhat," Ginny said. "One of those that's supposed to screen out all the harmful sun's rays. You know, the kind in the cancer society advertisements. It has to be pretty, too."

"I know exactly what you mean. I happen to have some right over here," Albert said. He walked over to the hat display. He pulled a couple hats off the display which he thought she would like and showed them to her. He held the ones she wanted to try on and replaced on the rack the ones she turned away.

"I told her she has plenty of hats," Helen said. "But she insisted on coming in here today and getting a new one." She clucked at her friend.

"Yes, this is what I want," Ginny said, pulling a brown cloth one off the rack. She looked about the store with a puzzled look and said, "Where's Lissa. She's such a dear girl. Isn't this her time to work?"

Albert fumbled with some items and shook his head.

"What?" Ginny said, putting the hat back down. "Is something wrong?"

"Lissa didn't come in to work today," Albert said. "And that's not at all like her. I tried calling her phone about an hour after her shift started but got no response."

"Oh dear," Ginny said. "You're right to be upset. She's a very responsible girl and is always here when she should be. I hope she's okay. We saw her just last night, didn't we Helen?" She looked at her friend for confirmation. "At the beach. She looked lovely."

"Yes, we did. She was on her way to meet a boyfriend. Craig Bergen. I think that's the name she told us. She stopped and talked to us for a few minutes. Ginny's right. She looked lovely. She was wearing the prettiest white outfit. Looked absolutely adorable."

"Craig Bergen. That's the name of the young man who came to the store here yesterday," Albert said. "Lissa told me all about him. She said she was meeting him at the beach last night. I have a bad feeling about this. I hope nothing has happened to her."

"Don't you think you should call someone?" Ginny asked. "The police or her parents again?"

"I'd call the police, but I don't think they'd do anything so soon," Albert said. "They usually wait a day or so because of runaways who go missing and then return. I'll try telephoning her family again, and if I don't get an answer, I'll drive over to her house. Just to be on the safe side."

"Good idea," Ginny said. "Do you want me to drive over to her house for you? I have the time, and I'd be happy to do that since you're working. I'm concerned about her."

"I'll go with you," Helen said. "Then, we'll call you, Albert, and let you know what we found out. And if she's at home sick or something, we'll have her telephone you to put your mind at ease. Okay? Either way, we'll get back to you."

"Okay," Albert said. "Let me get her file and I'll give you her address and phone number."

He retrieved a folder with Lissa's job application.

"She's only been working here a short time, but I feel as if I've known her a lot longer than that," Albert said, examining her application. He put an address and two phone numbers on a piece of paper and handed it to Ginny. "That's her address and phone number, and there's my cell phone number. Call me as soon as you know anything. Okay? Oh, and here's her parents' names." He took the paper back from her and wrote the names down.

Ginny looked at the address, 75 Blue Chameleon Circle, Palm Bay, and immediately recognized the area as a familiar one. "That's on the West side of I-95. Near where the fancy subdivision and new stores are," she said to Helen. "We've been through that section of town plenty of times."

"I'll call you as soon as we find something out," Ginny said to Albert.

The drive across the causeway and then south on Route One seemed to take longer than usual. Ginny turned right onto Malabar Road, following it under the I-95 overpass and continued until turning south onto Emerson Road.

"Now watch for house number 75," Ginny said as they slowly cruised along Blue Chameleon Circle. "Tell me when you see it."

Ginny kept her eyes on the road and managed the speed as slow as she could in case she needed to brake.

Helen gawked about, trying to see the house numbers.

"We're getting close," Helen said as they hit a straight stretch. "The odd numbers are on the right side. Sixty-nine, 71, 73, empty lot, 77."

"Wait a minute," Ginny said, stopping the car and backing up. "There's 73, then a vacant lot, then 77. There is no 75. It must be a mistake." She looked at the empty quarter acre. "Albert must have written the wrong number down." She backed up the car and stopped in front of the tangle of weeds where Lissa's home should have been. "Call him, Helen. He was upset and probably just wrote it down wrong."

Helen called Albert's cell phone.

Albert checked his records and told Helen that 75 Blue Chameleon Circle was the address Lissa wrote on her job application. He asked her to recite the address back to him to be sure she heard him.

"Are you suggesting I can't read or see the numbers right?" Helen asked, reminding him that she may be older but was not senile. "We're both wearing our glasses."

"No, no. I was just checking," Albert replied.

After ending the conversation, Albert muttered aloud to no one in particular, "I should have gone myself."

Ginny scrutinized the large undeveloped piece of land. It was overgrown with wild ferns, palms, shrubs, and invasive pepper trees. The tangled vegetation was enough that a person would be hard pressed to get through it without crawling. It was obvious that a home had never occupied that weedy space.

"Let's stop at one of the houses next to the lot and find out if anyone has ever heard of this young girl or her family," Helen said. "We have the names of her parents written here. We'll see if these people know them." She peered closely at the list through her trifocals.

No one had heard of a Lissa Powell or her parents. Nor did they ever see on their street, anyone matching Lissa's description.

Ginny phoned Albert, who gave them another piece of news. He had contacted City Hall and was informed that there was no other street in the city with the name Blue Chameleon Circle, so they were in the right neighborhood.

"When you report this to the police," Ginny said, "If they think I can be of any help, send them to my home." *I know exactly what to tell them.*

Ginny made another phone call to tell someone she was finished with her part of the Play and was going home.

As soon as he finished talking with Ginny and Helen, Albert changed his mind about waiting to report Lissa missing. He called the police department. He gave them Lissa's full name and explained to them the concern he and the others had about her disappearance. He included the information of her perfect work record, where she was going last evening, and how he got no answer at her home phone number. He also recounted Ginny and Helen's experience when trying to locate Lissa's house. His report included his observations that Lissa was a good girl, not the type to run off somewhere like some other teenagers with whom they dealt.

Officer Lopez telephoned Albert an hour after his call to the station and promised to look into his concerns. She arrived at the surf shop shortly thereafter.

"This is a copy of her job application," Albert said, handing the policewoman some papers. "I also have a recent picture of Lissa taken here at the shop. She asked me to take the photograph shortly after she started to work here. Said she wanted to send it to some friends. She gave me a copy, and I kept it with her file."

Lopez observed the color photo of the teenager. In it, Lissa was looking down and to the left, and the print was out of focus a little bit.

"Pretty girl from what I can see. Red hair," Lopez said. "Is this the best picture of her that you have? It's not a very good one."

"Yes, I know it's not too good, but it's all I have. Our store cameras have somehow been erased so we can't use them. As I told you, she was a responsible girl and very nice. Respectful. You know what I mean?"

The officer shook her head yes. She was touched by the employer's concern for his salesgirl.

"How tall would you say she is?" Lopez asked.

"About five feet seven inches tall. And even though she went to the beach every morning, she was white-skinned. Just had a little tan. Not much."

"And you say you tried locating her home and telephoning her family," Lopez said.

"Yes. I've been trying her phone number all afternoon. And a couple of my customers drove to her address to make sure she was all right since we couldn't get her on the phone. When they went to her street address, all that was there was a vacant lot and none of the neighbors recognized the name as someone who lived in their neighborhood. And they claimed not to have ever seen anyone on their street matching Lissa's description."

"What was her state of mind yesterday when she was here working? Was she upset? Did she mention a fight with her parents or a boyfriend? Any problems at school? Did she do drugs?" The policewoman wrote as she spoke. "I have to ask these questions."

"She was fine. She worked her shift," Albert said. "She was excellent with the customers and made a lot of sales yesterday, as usual. She wasn't upset. Quite the contrary. She was her usual happy self. She was excited. I had just given her a raise. And she was happy because she was supposed to meet a boyfriend at the beach at 8:30 last night. Ginny Anderson, the lady that went looking for Lissa, lives near the beach. She said she saw Lissa all dressed up last evening, walking on the boardwalk, going to meet the boy. His name is Bergen, by the way. Craig Bergen. Lissa told me all about him yesterday."

He paused. "I don't think Lissa did drugs, Officer. She just didn't strike me as that kind of a person. Frankly, she wasn't like any of the other teenagers I have had working here in the past. She was more mature."

"I've got the information down and will make some inquiries to see if we can locate her. It's too soon to put out a missing person on her, but with your description of what has happened and the kind of employee you say she was, I'm uncomfortable about waiting too long on this. Can I take this photo with me?" she asked, holding it up.

"Sure. Her social security number, parents' names, everything I have on her is on your copy of the job application," Albert said. "Take that, too, if it will help. Oh, yeah. Ginny Anderson and her friends' addresses are listed on this note card. They told me to tell you to stop by to talk to them if you think it would help find Lissa. Mrs. Anderson said she was going to ask some of the neighbors to help her walk the beach to look for the girl. They have a Neighborhood Watch Group they're involved with who are going to help them."

"That's good. The watch group has been trained not to touch anything they find, so they'll know what to do. What do you know about this boyfriend she was meeting? Craig Bergen?" Lopez asked.

"Not much," Albert said. "Just what Lissa told me." He repeated everything she had said about Bergen.

"He was here yesterday talking to her. Bought some things, too. Paid cash. As I said, our in-store surveillance tape would have helped, because Lissa would have been on that tape, too, but it's no good now. I can give you our copy of the outside corner surveillance tape if you want. There's a good shot of Bergen on that from when he left the store."

Lopez thanked him and viewed the tape Albert had. It was not a good image but would have to suffice.

"I hadn't noticed it at the time, but it looks as if he was avoiding being taped," Albert said. "He had those sunglasses on most of the time, too, which makes it difficult to get a good view of his face. I don't like the way this is shaping up, Officer. I'm concerned about Lissa."

"This whole situation is a concern to me, too. And that Bergen guy looks very familiar. Like I've seen him before. "

Lopez finished interviewing Albert and promised to get back to him if she learned anything. The officer did not feel too worried about the young girl, knowing most of these missing kids ended up being runaways. She reminded Albert of that. Still, her gut reaction about Lissa Powell was one of some alarm.

"I have to say again that I just don't think her being a runaway is the case here," Albert replied. "It just doesn't add up. Someone ought to go talk to that Bergen guy. See what he has to say."

"Do you know where he lives?" Lopez asked.

"Ginny says he lives at The Banana Motel on A1A. She's seen him around at the beach, surfing and hanging out."

"The Banana Motel is an odd place for an 18-year-old and his family to live, don't you think? That motel caters mostly to tourists, and the rooms aren't very spacious or even outfitted to house a family."

Albert walked the policewoman to the door and thanked her for looking into this so quickly. "Please call me or come back to the store anytime if you think it would help," he said. "I'll do what I can."

Officer Lopez got into her police car and checked in with her supervisor. She put some data into the computer and was surprised when Lissa's social security number came up invalid. It was a fake ID. She called her supervisor again, gave him the boyfriend's name and address to check on in their database, and asked for backup to go to The Banana Motel to find Craig Bergen. She also requested an officer go to the beach area to join the Neighborhood Watch Group already there . . . just in case.

CHAPTER SIX

At The Banana Motel...

With the heavy traffic flow, it took Officer Lopez longer than usual to get to The Banana Motel. True to its name, it was a bright yellow three-story place of business with a banana-shaped neon sign out front advertising vacancies. She guessed it must have been built in the fifties, given the boxy structure and dated style. Multi-storied, modern complexes flanked the motel, accentuating its age.

Her backup, Officers Darrell Tucker and Clark Edwards arrived together within a few minutes. They parked their police car at the front of the motel and got out, walked over to Lopez's car and rapped on the window.

Lopez briefed the men on everything she had so far on Lissa's disappearance and her gut feeling of the importance of moving quickly to find Bergen.

The police entered the motel at the front of the building.

"Hi, officers. What can I do for you today?" the desk clerk asked. "Is something wrong?"

"Routine check, Mr. Patel," Lopez said, reading the clerk's name-tag. "Do you have a Mr. Craig Bergen staying here?"

"Yes, we do. Please call me John." He smiled. "Bergen has been here for at least three weeks. Let me check to make sure." The clerk tapped some buttons on the computer and read from the screen.

"Yes. He came in three weeks ago. Pays weekly. Stays in room 24." He looked blankly at the officers. "Is something wrong? Is he in trouble?"

"Is he alone or are his parents with him?" Lopez asked.

"Parents?" the clerk said. "No. He lives here by himself. Quiet. No trouble. Spends most of the day with his surfboard at the beach. What's this about? Is he in some sort of trouble?"

"We have some routine questions to ask him. Please show us where his room is," Lopez said.

"Sure," John said. "Follow me." He pulled a key from a board on the back wall and yelled to someone in the back room. "Al. Can you watch the front desk for a few minutes? I have some officers here who want to talk to one of our customers."

Al came out from behind the curtained doorway and gave the police a worried once-over. He looked at John and nervously tapped his chubby fingers together in front of him.

"Is something wrong?" Al asked in a thick accent. "Has something happened? Is it about those missing bleach bottle things?" He kept tapping his fingers. "What is it? What's wrong?" He rubbed his hands across an expanse of stomach.

"No, it's not the missing bleach. Not that I know of," John said. "The officers just want to talk with Craig Bergen, room 24. Watch the desk. I'll be right back."

Al nodded his head but retained his worried expression. He wrung his hands, then tapped his fingers together. He looked back and forth from John to the officers and mumbled about the bleach. He frowned when he saw the two marked cars parked out front. He wanted the police cars moved to the back, away from where potential customers could see them.

John took the lead and motioned for the police to follow him.

"Very hot again today," John said. "Good beach day." He looked up at the beautiful blue Florida sky with its puffy white clouds. "No rain coming again."

"Yes, very hot," Lopez said. "But we need the rain."

Room 24 was at the back of the three-story block building, near an alcove where outside stairs went up to the next level. There was a white plastic lawn chair to the left of the door to Bergen's room. It was at least another 400 feet to the beach behind them. A path meandered through an open area, through some low vegetation, then, obscured, down to the shore.

The officers remained alert, looking about while the clerk knocked on the door and loudly called out Bergen's name.

"I don't think he's here," John said, putting his ear up to the door. "I don't hear anything."

Officer Lopez stepped up, knocked on the door and yelled, "Bergen. Craig Bergen. Are you in there? It's the police. We have some questions to ask you. Open the door." She stepped back, hand on her holstered gun.

There was no answer.

She looked back at the path leading to the beach area. The first stretch was open with the remaining length of path unseen because of sea grape bushes and native plantings. The vegetation obscured their view of the ocean, which could be heard rushing to shore in the background. Overhead, terns were flying toward the water, screeching at unseen concerns.

"Keep a watch out for Bergen," Lopez said to the clerk. "Let us know if you see him coming."

John nodded his head. "It's hot," he said again, seemingly not knowing what else to say.

Lopez was about to touch the doorknob when she stopped. She leaned over to get a better look at a red smear on the door where the doorknob was attached. "What does that look like to you?" she said to her fellow officers, stepping back for them to see. Her gut was churning as she thought of the lovely young Lissa.

Darrell peered at the smear. "Some kind of a red smudge. Looks like dried blood, but I can't be sure. What do you think, Clark?" He backed away.

His partner took his turn and said, "Looks like dried blood to me, too. And I see a fingerprint in it." He pointed at the knob.

"No," the desk clerk said in disbelief. His eyes got large. He was mopping his face and neck with a kerchief. "No," he said again. He looked at the police, dumbfounded. "We never have trouble here. Never. I run a good establishment."

"And what's that smell?" Lopez said, sniffing at the door jamb. "Bleach. It smells strong of bleach in there." She turned to John. "You sure Bergen isn't in here?"

"Sorta sure," John said. "He stopped by the desk earlier to get a newspaper and said he was going to the beach. He spends a lot of time there. Sometimes he tells us about all the pretty girls he sees." He smiled. Then, glancing at the blood, he frowned.

"Tucker, call the office and tell them what we've got here. Tell them to send the CSI Detectives here now. Clark and I will secure the room." Lopez said.

John was instructed to keep away from the door and not to touch anything. He cooperated immediately, muttering unintelligibly under his breath about being hot. He complained about needing to get out of the sun.

Tucker went to the front of the building to his car and leaned against it. He spoke into the mic on his sleeve.

Lopez ushered everyone into the alcove behind the stairs. They leaned beside an ice-maker and some vending machines so to not be seen by anyone walking up from the ocean. She didn't want Craig to be alarmed by their presence should he come by. Perspiring heavily, she was glad to be out of the hot sun, too.

The officers were watching the beach path for signs of their target. The wind whistled through the plantings and for awhile, all they saw were sea oats swaying in the breeze.

The first person walking the path from the beach toward the motel was an older man with dark, wrinkled skin. His skinny legs followed down to large sandaled feet. A cigar was clenched between his large lips. It kept moving up and down as he walked and hummed a tune.

Lopez looked over to John. He shook his head. Attentive to the action, he was watching everything play out before him. *Stick to the script. The Play must be followed.*

A tanned young man in a swimsuit and white tee shirt was next to come out of the thick shrubs toward the motel. He was carrying a yellow surfboard. Strolling leisurely, it was apparent he had not spotted the officers.

Lopez looked to John for a positive ID, her eyes darting from him to the male.

John indicated it was Bergen. He mopped his face and neck again with his kerchief and backed as far away from the group as he could.

The policewoman, her fingers to her lips for everyone to be quiet, spoke softly into her phone for Darrell to rejoin them. She called the station for more backup, apprising them that Bergen was in sight and heading for the motel.

Darrell crept behind the motel to the vending machines. He slowly walked to where Lopez was hidden.

After Bergen passed the alcove by his motel room door, he stopped and jammed the bottom of his surfboard into some sand. The police officers stepped out from the shadows while their quarry was reaching for his room key which was pinned inside his swimsuit pocket.

"What's up, Officers?" Craig said, flashing his handsome grin. He was nervously looking at them, sweat beads dripping from his hairline. He attempted to back away a few feet.

The officers shifted their weight to keep him within their circle. "I'm Officer Lopez, and we have a few questions to ask you." Seeing Bergen up close, the experienced officer assessed his age to be more in his twenties than in his teens.

"What's this about?" Bergen asked, perspiration rolling down his neck, wetting the neckline of his shirt. Damp circles spotted the fabric under his armpits like half moons.

"We're trying to locate a young girl named Lissa Powell. A 17-year-old redhead. You were seen talking with her on several occasions. And we have witnesses who claim you were to meet with her at the beach last night. Do you know where she is?" Lopez said.

"He had a redhead here at the motel with him last night," John whispered to Lopez, leaning in closer to get his message across.

She acknowledged she heard him.

Seeing Officer Lopez briefly occupied, Bergen made a move. He bent down and tried to get between her and Clark, thinking he could maybe take down the woman, the smallest of the three. Bergen was not about to stay around for the questions and their discovering his real name.

As Bergen was ducking and darting away, Darrell reached long arms out and got a piece of his tee shirt. The damp fabric tore away as Bergen took off running straight toward the beach path.

Off balance, Darrell fell to one knee, caught himself with his left hand, and pushed up to get free from the sand.

Clark reached out to help him and the two of them got slowed down from the chase.

Bergen's sandals flew off, and he strayed from the path into loose sand. The further he went, the more he got bogged down in the hot, soft sand hindering his pace. He struggled and cursed, arms flailing to gain some sort of balance. "If you come near me, I'll kill you," he said to the officers.

Lopez sprinted well ahead of the other policemen, lunged, and wrapped her arms tightly around Bergen's bare lower legs for a tackle, the likes of which any NFL player would have been proud.

Her quarry dropped hard, face-down into a large bougainvillea bush.

Screaming from the pain of thorns piercing his chest and face, Bergen wrestled with the smaller officer. He tried to grab her gun, but she beat his hands away. The more he twisted and turned, the tighter she held on. She bested him every time.

Lopez was in her element.

Unbeknownst to Bergen, the officer's grip strength was legendary in the local police force. He felt the full effect of that legend now.

Darrell and Clark recovered and were on him in a flurry of sand and vegetation. They grabbed Bergen's arms and pinned them behind him. Darrell cuffed their prisoner's hands and pulled him to his feet.

Bergen sputtered and spit, complaining about his skin hurting.

Darrell bent down to rub his sore left knee and noticed he had torn his pants when he fell. "You're gonna pay for these," he said to Bergen. The officer brushed sand from himself, keeping one hand on the prisoner.

Clark was breathing heavily from the chase and bent over to catch his breath, his hands on his knees. "I gotta lose some weight," he gasped.

Lopez snickered, wiped sand from her uniform, and checked to see that her equipment was okay. Satisfied that nothing was missing or broken, she tightened her grip on the suspect. "Threatening to kill police officers is not so smart, Bergen," she said.

All of the officers' short-sleeved uniforms were damp and still had bits of sand on them from the tussle. Their caps had fallen off, and their hair was mussed.

"I'll get those for you," John said. The motel manager retrieved the officers' caps for them, brushed them off, and carried them with him. Looking satisfied with the outcome, he followed behind the group. *This is going well. Daddy will be pleased.*

Bergen was escorted to the front of his motel room and placed in the white plastic lawn chair, arms cuffed behind him. Small pieces of his ripped tee shirt hung off his neck. He was panting and angry.

"What do you think you're doing?" the young man said. "I haven't done anything."

"Shut up," Lopez said.

She asked the manager, "Where's the key?"

John, unnerved by the events, handed her the motel's master key. He stepped away from the door area.

"Thank you," Lopez said. "Don't go anywhere. And where are those detectives I called for?"

Al came out the side entrance from the front desk to see what was going on but was told by John to go back to the office and get their first aid kit for Bergen's wounds.

Al wrung his hands and rushed inside, muttering to himself in his native tongue.

"Get me a freakin' doctor," Bergen said. "Can't you see I'm hurt?" Small droplets of blood were oozing from inflamed puncture wounds on his upper chest and face. "I'll sue your asses off for this."

"We're not interested in anymore of your threats," Lopez said. "We have enough probable cause to search the room now. Blood on the door and a sighting of a redhead matching the description of a missing girl seen here with you last night. We're going in. She could be in there now. Hurt, or worse."

"What redhead in my room? Who said that?" Bergen said. "That's a lie."

"Listen up. Pay attention to Darrell, here. He's gonna read you your rights," Lopez said.

Darrell recited the Miranda, speaking loud and clear to avoid any misunderstandings.

Bergen indicated he understood and told the officer to get lost. He struggled with the handcuffs behind him in a futile attempt to remove them. "Take these off. I haven't done anything wrong."

Another police cruiser screeched into the motel parking lot. Doors opened and CSI Detectives got out. Carrying their gear, they approached Officer Lopez.

She brought them up to date on what information they had, and the Detectives began their investigation.

Inside the motel office, Al slapped his hand against his forehead and let out an expletive when he heard the sirens and saw more flashing lights. "Bad for business, Bad for business," he said. He rushed the first aid kit to his boss.

The detectives donned plastic gloves and used the key to unlock Bergen's room. When the door swung aside, an unmistakable whiff of bleach greeted them. It was strong enough to make them back away. They kept the door wide open for a few minutes to air it out.

"Now we know where the stolen bleach got to," John said loudly to no one in particular. "Yep. That's where my stolen bleach got to." He pointed an accusing finger at Craig Bergen.

"What stolen bleach, you liar. What are you talking about?"

Their firearms drawn, the Detectives sucked in fresh air and entered the room.

"Lissa Powell. Are you in here?" one officer said, swinging his gun back and forth as he moved forward.

No answer.

"Lissa, it's the police. We're here to help you. It's okay. You're safe now. Come on out."

They searched the room, looking under the bed and behind the furniture. Within the small room, there weren't too many places for someone to secret themselves, or to be hidden.

"She's not in here," an office yelled to Lopez and the others. He continued looking around.

"I could have told you that," Bergen said. "Stupid cops. I never had a redhead in my room. What a bunch of losers."

Lopez looked at the motel manager who nodded his head and mouthed 'Yes, there was.'

One of the officers guarding Bergen opened the first aid kit Al had handed him. Pulling things out and sorting through them, he was deciding what to use.

"Here, I'll do that," John said, taking it from his hands. "That way, you can watch your prisoner. Do you want me to put something on those wounds?" he said to Bergen as he removed the cap from a tube of ointment.

"You better believe I do. It hurts bad. I'm gonna sue you. All of you guys," he said to the officers and the clerk. "I want a doctor, and I want my lawyer. We're looking at police brutality here. They'll arrest all of you, and if they don't, I'll get you."

John put some ointment on a piece of square gauze and patted some on the open areas. While the others were occupied looking elsewhere, he also took something out of his pocket and applied scant traces of it to Bergen's hands.

The angry prisoner was so upset he hardly noticed what the clerk was doing under the guise of helping him.

"I said I want to speak to my lawyer. Are you guys deaf or what?"

"Keep your shirt on," Clark said back. Spying the tattered tee shirt, he laughed a little then regained his official look.

Detectives continued processing the scene while the officers watched and took turns keeping Bergen in his chair.

Across the street...

A car was stopped with the lone occupant observing the events at the motel.

"Look, I can see something going down here and I don't like it," the occupant rasped into his phone. "I can't do this by myself. I need more help, or we'll never keep up with this group."

At Daddy's office...

"Hi, Backer," Daddy said.

"Hi, yourself. How's it going?"

"Right on schedule. I heard from John. The Antagonist is cuffed, and the evidence is being collected," Daddy said.

"Great. Call me when the Play is finished."

"Will do," Daddy said.

"Before you hang up, I have something important to tell you," the Backer said. "There's a mole in our midst. I don't know who it is, but he's working with a government committee. My sources tell me law enforcement at its highest level has put a task force together to find out how some crimes, through our Plays, have been solved. They're worried about convictions being thrown out due to outside influences and tainted evidence, and also vigilante movements subverting the justice system. They are focused on something called the Theater Group. So far, they know the name we operate under, and a little bit about our structure. They even know someone in the Group is called 'Daddy,' although they don't know who you are. They have a dated description of you but not a picture. This is worrisome. I think I can eliminate it, but it's worrisome. Any idea who the problem person is?"

Daddy was surprised and concerned. He searched his thoughts for clues to the identity of their traitor.

"No," Daddy said. "I'm caught off guard. I'll have to give it some thought. What do you think? Any ideas?"

"As I said, I'm not sure, but I think we need to take action with several of your closest confidantes in the Group. It has to be someone who knows you fairly well. Someone who has knowledge on how the Group is run. Someone you trust. We can't let them get your fingerprints. Are you still wearing the fake prints we had made?"

"Yes, I am. I use them whenever I send files out or the rare times I meet with people in person. "

"Good," the Backer said. "At least the mole won't have your real prints. The new ones our fabricator came up with are the best. They're lightweight, easy to apply and remove, and almost impossible to detect. Very realistic."

"I know. I almost forget I have them on," Daddy said. "And I don't seem to be allergic to them, although I think Lissa is. She's been rubbing her fingertips where they were attached."

"We'll have someone take a look at her fingers just to make sure she's okay. Be careful, Daddy, and let me know if you think of anything that would lead us to the mole. Don't take any unnecessary chances. We need to stop whoever it is. And we must do it now."

"Thank you for the information. I'll be careful," Daddy said. "Keep me posted on what you learn, and I'll contact you if I have any ideas about this. One more thing. Benny thought he was being followed recently. He managed to lose them, but that incident might be related to the mole."

"Yes, it might. I'll call Benny and discuss it with him. Talk to you soon," the Backer said. He hung up the phone, more than a little concerned about Daddy and the Theater Group, the focus of his life and fortune.

Daddy felt an uneasiness creeping over him. *Someone in my few trusted top confidantes is a mole. Who could it be?* He made a mental list of the few names and faces of people who have almost daily contact with him in one way or another. The mole had to be someone who knows what he looks like, who saw him sometime without a disguise. He narrowed it down to three people and didn't want to believe it was one of them.

CHAPTER SEVEN

Later that week...

"Yes, I found it," Ginny said. "At the edge of the beach, lodged in some sea grass in the sand dune. The same day they picked up Craig, er, Karl Blass. Imagine!" She cringed at the thought of Lissa's boyfriend Craig Bergen turning out to be Karl Blass, the serial murder suspect known to the police and the press as 'The Beach Boy.'

"I get the chills just thinking about it," Ginny said. "I can hardly bear knowing that Lissa was 'The Beach Boy's' date on the night she went missing. It's horrible. All of it. And where is she?"

Everyone who read about 'The Beach Boy' agreed it was terrible that their charming community had been the temporary home of the infamous murderer. They were horrified that while the police and others had been looking for him up and down the east coast, he had been at their beachside community at The Banana Motel, a respected, well-run facility.

"We didn't touch the shoe when we found it, did we, Helen?" Ginny said, looking over at her friend. "We didn't fool with the evidence. We know better. We've been very well trained."

"No, we didn't touch a thing. We have witnesses to prove it," Helen said. "We watch enough television to know not to do that.

And we've worked with the Neighborhood Watch Group before. Ginny and I know what we're doing. And she's right. We're well trained."

"Are you sure it was Lissa's?" Albert said. "Maybe it belonged to another girl. A lot of the teens are wearing that particular style of shoes. My own teenage daughters wear them."

"We're pretty sure. And that's what we told the police officers when they went to retrieve it. She was wearing gray ballet-style slippers with strings of pretty beads on them. They were laced up her legs that night. She lifted her skirt to show them to us. We're positive it's hers. We were lucky to have found it. It was Helen's idea to go looking. We went along the beach and looked around. Some of the Neighborhood Watch Group joined us, and we walked across the sand from the sea oats to the ocean. Anyway, when we spotted her shoe in the grass, I called the group to join us so they could witness that we didn't touch it. I telephoned the police, and we stayed right there guarding it until they arrived so no one else would touch it either. I'm rather proud of all of us."

"She must have taken them off when she was walking along the water with Bergen. I mean Karl Blass, so they wouldn't get wet," Helen said. "It's so confusing. I'm going to call him Karl Blass from now on."

"Me, too. That's his real name," Ginny said. "I told the policemen the same thing you did, Helen. That Lissa must have taken them off so as not to soil them when she was walking with Blass."

"I suppose the police interviewed you then," Albert said. "Since you two were the last people to see Lissa alive. Besides Blass," he added. "I hate saying it like that. It sounds as if he killed her."

"I know what you mean. It sounds final. I don't like it." Ginny said. "And yes, the police did come to my home and interview me. After they bagged the shoe and finished searching the beach, they walked to my house and asked a lot of questions. We told them everything we knew. Like, how excited Lissa was to be meeting him. Everything she said about him. What she was wearing. What time we saw her. Everything. We even showed them where she was standing when we spoke with her that night. Before they left, they said they were going to dust the shoe for fingerprints to confirm it was the same one Lissa had on."

"The police already came here and checked her locker and some other items she touched for her prints. I suppose they'll compare them to any prints they find on the shoe. See if they match," Albert said. "They fingerprinted all of us, too."

"This is all very upsetting," she said. "I don't know what to make of it."

"The officers took her things from her locker," Albert said. "Some personal items, like her beach bag with her swimsuit and towel, were gone. She must have taken them with her the last time she worked here. I sure hope that whatever they got helps bring that killer to justice."

"What I can't understand is where Lissa lived," Helen said. "And where are her parents? No one has come forth to claim her. Even after the newspaper articles on her. We're hoping someone will recognize her."

"I wish I knew the answers to those questions. The police are convinced she was a runaway from another part of Florida. Or maybe even another state. Why else would she give us a fake social security number and address?" Albert said.

"I can't think of any reason she would do that," Ginny said. "Unless it's like the police believe, and she was a runaway. I hope they fry that Karl Blass."

"Me, too," Helen said.

"I'm trying to keep an open mind, but the evidence against him is growing," Albert said. "Especially since they checked his fingerprints and found out who he really is, 'The Beach Boy' killer. Everyone was looking for him. He got off for that murder in New Jersey. Then his DNA or a sighting of him turned up where more girls were murdered or missing. All either at the beach or nearby. And that crazy twist about the ice cream. It turns up at the crime scenes. Weird."

"A couple of the other girls were redheads, too, according to the paper," Helen said. "He must have had a thing for young redheads."

"He'll be sorry he came to Florida," Ginny said. "We have capital punishment here and aren't afraid to use it."

"That's right," Helen said. "Ted Bundy won't be murdering any more women now."

"Blass won't get any sympathy from me," Ginny said, her eyes misting over. "I'm telling you, I hope he gets the death penalty." She shuddered.

Helen noticed that was the second time her friend had said that and said, "I'm sorry, Ginny. This must be terribly hard for you. Given what happened to your Bobby and all." She patted her friend's hand.

Helen and Albert shared sympathetic glances, remembering how Ginny's only child, Bobby, was found murdered a few years ago. In his late thirties, Bobby was knifed for the $25 he had in his pocket. His killer, Glen Spade, accosted the young man on his way home from a convenience store. Two eyewitnesses pointed the finger at Spade, a local drug dealer. Spade's fingerprints were all over Bobby from when he rifled his pockets. Spade said he did that after finding Bobby already dead. He was put on trial but got off because the chief witness recanted her testimony, refusing to talk during the trial, and the second witness left town for parts unknown.

"I manage to do what I have to do and make my peace with that," Ginny said. "I had to, to keep from going crazy. Glen Spade can't live forever and justice will be served in the after-life. Although, I would love to witness him getting what he has coming to him here and now. I would pay anything to make that happen." Her eyes became hard. "Anything."

At the Brevard County Sheriff's jail...

"You're gonna have to help me, here, Blass, if I'm going to help you," Attorney Tyler Graham said, leaning in to his client. "I need to know the truth about what happened that night on the beach. You have to tell me everything again. Leave nothing out." He leaned on the desk.

"I told you the truth," Blass hissed. "Nothing happened. I've been set up. That's what happened."

His counsel rolled his eyes and closed a folder he had opened. *How many times have I heard that lame excuse?*

"Hey," Blass shouted. "If you don't believe me then get out of here. I need a lawyer who's behind me all the way." He glared at his

52

attorney. "And I want to sue that officer who threw me into the thorn bushes. Some of the wounds are infected. If the clerk hadn't put ointment on me, it would have been worse." Blass opened his shirt, exposing welts and sores on his chest.

"The officers say that she tackled you," his lawyer said. "You were running away from her. There were eye witnesses."

"Liars," Blass said. "She pretended to tackle me but instead pushed me into the thorn bush. Do you think a stupid woman could tackle me? No way. She pushed me." He buttoned his shirt back up. "She'll pay for that."

"Watch your mouth, Blass," Tyler said. "That's a threat against a police officer. You'll find yourself in more trouble than you already are. There were quite a few eye witnesses who saw her tackle you. But I don't want to argue about that now. We don't have much time here, so let's go over your story again. You were supposed to meet Lissa at 8:30 that night, right?" Tyler said. "Then what happened?"

"Right," Blass said. "I was to meet her at 8:30 p.m. I went down to the beach where we said we would meet. I got there about 8:15. It was dark out, and no one else was around. I kept checking my watch 'cuz I was looking forward to seeing her. She's a good-looking girl." He grinned. "Just what I was looking for."

"A bit young for you, wouldn't you say?" Tyler said. "I mean, you're 24 years old, and she was only 17."

"Hey, can I help it she thought I was a lot younger?" Blass said. "I appeal to women of all ages."

His attorney let that slide.

"Did you tell her you were 18 years old?" Tyler asked. "That's what the witnesses are saying. Lissa told them you said you were 18. That you lived at the motel with your parents since your house was being remodeled and wasn't finished yet. Any of that sound familiar? What was that about? You don't have any family in this state. You don't even own a house here. And you haven't worked any job long enough to earn any money to buy one, let alone remodel it."

"Lies. All of it. Lies. They're all lying. Lissa, the cops, all of them."

Despite the tough talk he was dishing out, Blass was pretty shook. *She must have blabbed everything she knew. I didn't think she'd do that. I'll have to be more careful in the future. Take them down before they can talk.*

"She must have misunderstood me," Blass said. "Geez, do I look 18? I mean I look really good, but not 18."

"Yes, you do. And that's the wrong question to ask," his attorney said. "Don't ever ask that of anyone. Especially if you get on the stand. Because, with your face and physique, you could look 18. Have you forgotten already the trial I got you through up north in Atlantic City? 'The Beach Boy,' the press and police called you. You were 20 then and told Charlotte you were 16. The story you told Lissa is very similar to what you told that girl. And the circumstances surrounding this girl's disappearance are way too close to that case for comfort. The police are smart. They're going to use that against you."

"What are you saying? You're supposed to be on my side. I was found not guilty. Remember? A nice jury let me go."

"I still can't believe you got off. If we wouldn't have challenged the handling of the DNA evidence and created doubt, who knows what would have happened? Those bleeding-heart liberals on the jury bought the story of your sad, abusive childhood, or they would have looked at the evidence a lot closer. And you would have been convicted and locked up."

Tyler harbored uncomfortable feelings about his contribution to enabling a murderer to get off, only to kill again and again. Assuring that a murderous client's rights are not violated during proceedings had been personally costly to him, and he didn't know if he could continue doing so.

"I passed the polygraph, remember? I didn't kill Charlotte. I told you then, and I'm telling you that now. I'm innocent, and the jury knew it. And I didn't kill Lissa, either. I don't know where she is. The police don't even know if that's her real name," Blass said. "Come on. Let's do the lie detector test."

"They're not going to offer you a lie detector test this time. They looked into your past record and saw where you beat it several times when they knew you were guilty, so they're not going to ask for it. I might, though," Tyler said. "Even if it's not admissible in court, it looks good on the news when you pass it. Of course, you know that sociopaths can answer questions about their guilt without becoming anxious or sweating so they pass the test."

Blass smiled. "What does being a sociopath have to do with me? It's a good idea for me to take that test. I know I can ace it again. Let's do it today. Now."

"We'll see. Let's get back to the night you were supposed to meet Lissa," Tyler said. "How long did you hang around waiting for her at the beach?"

"Like I said, I got there at 8:15 p.m. She was supposed to arrive at 8:30. I stayed there until 9:30. It was nice out that night, so I didn't mind the wait."

"Why'd you wait around so long? Most guys would have left after a half-hour," Tyler said. "I know I would have."

"I told you she was worth waiting for. And she told me she might be late and to wait for her, so I hung out," Blass said. "She said she was going to have dinner with her parents and wanted to meet me after that. So, I stayed. Besides, we were meeting right behind the motel where I was staying." He shrugged his shoulders. "I coulda' waited all night, really." He regretted losing his prey.

"You are aware that Lissa had no parents that anyone knew of?" Tyler said. "So she couldn't have had dinner with them. The police went to the address she gave her employer, and it's a vacant lot. Nothing. No house, no family. Even her social security number was false. Not only do we not know where she is, we don't know anything about her." He tapped his pencil on the desk. "The police think she was probably a runaway from another state, living here for the summer. What do you think of that?"

Blass was beginning to realize how bad that made him look and was starting to feel sorry for himself.

"That little liar. She told me she went to a Catholic High School. That she lived on the mainland all her life, and that she had chores to do after dinner so she might be late for our date. I believed her. What a stinking liar."

"One liar talking to another, Blass. That's no defense. According to witnesses, you told her you just graduated from a charter school. And that you were going to attend Auburn University in the fall." He smirked, thinking this bum couldn't get into a high school let alone a college. He leaned his head back and looked up at the ceiling, overwhelmed how the case was stacked against his client.

Blass was thinking about Lissa. She puzzled him, and he wondered how could he have made such a poor choice for a victim. *What a big-mouth stupid broad.*

"No. I never said that. I never told her any of those things. She made all that up. You already know she lied about where she lived and stuff. Stinking damn liar. Geez, you can't trust anyone these days."

"Well, that's what more than one witness is saying. So tell me, did anyone see you down at the beach that night? Anyone who can say you were there alone until 9:30?"

"It was dark out, what'd ya' expect? There aren't any lights on the beach. You know that. Because of the stupid turtles hatching. Who cares about the turtles anyway? I'd kill 'em if I found any." Blass was getting frustrated.

Tyler frowned at the cruel comment. "Stick to what happened that night. Answer me. Did anyone see you at the beach that night?"

"No, no one saw me. Not that I know of. I waited for Lissa until 9:30. Then I went back to the motel. Ask John Patel. He'll tell you. He saw me."

"He saw you, all right. Patel says he saw you go to your motel room at 9 o'clock. With a redhead."

"That lying foreigner." He was getting flustered. "He and everyone else is against me. They planned this."

"He's not a foreigner. He's an American citizen. He said when he went past your door he heard the two of you in there. Then, when he took his break at 10, you were gone. That's what he told the police."

"He's lying, I'm telling you. It was about 9:35. I know because I looked at my watch. I came to the door of my room. Alone. John was at the soda machine, getting a soda. I said hello. He said hello back. That was it. End of story."

"John tells a different version. He says it was after midnight when he saw you come back in. He wasn't sure of the exact time but knows it was after midnight because he went to get a soda from the machine at that time. It's all very clear to John, because he doesn't usually stay that late at the motel but worked overtime that night." Tyler looked disgusted. "So you're telling me that everyone is lying but you. All of these law-abiding citizens are lying. Is that it?"

"Yes," Blass said. "That's what I'm telling you. I know what happened. Give me the polygraph. They're framing me, and I can prove it by taking the polygraph."

"That won't work. I told you. You hurt yourself with that one. The police know you can beat it. They won't allow it in the courtroom. The only good it will do is that it will look great in the press. We need more than a polygraph test to prove you're innocent. We need some evidence in your favor."

"I'm telling you the truth," Blass said. "You're my lawyer. It's your job to get me off."

"I need more than what we've got so far. Now," Tyler said. "Let me remind you that witnesses said that they spoke with Lissa at 8:30 when she was on the boardwalk on her way to meet you. Two nice little old ladies, Blass. They had a conversation with her. They can recite it verbatim. Lissa told them she was meeting you, going by the false name of Craig Bergen, at 8:30. That she was excited to be seeing you. They asked her if it was the same young man who lived at The Banana Motel. The same guy who goes surfing at the beach every day. She said yes. The witnesses told the police exactly what she was wearing. White blouse, white skirt, gray ballerina shoes. They saw her go down the steps to the beach. Two little old ladies, Blass. Well-respected women of the community. Are you going to call two little old ladies liars?" He was getting frustrated with his client. "How could you not have seen her on the beach that night when two gray haired ladies saw her? She was wearing white. You couldn't miss her. Help me out here."

"Me help you out? What are you talking about? You're supposed to help me out. I'm telling you I never saw her. Someone else must have gotten to her first. And who are those two lyin' old bags? I don't know them. How do they know me?"

"Don't ever talk about them like that," Tyler said. "Listen to yourself. It makes you sound guilty of something. At the very least, you sound crass."

"I'm guilty of a lot of things," Blass said. "But not this. Come on, I didn't do this. And I don't care what any of them say. I'm innocent. How many times do I have to tell you?"

The thought of doing jail time was causing him to imagine what his future would be like inside a prison. He worried he'd be a sitting duck for the prisoners - or worse, he could be executed.

"Then explain the rest of the evidence to me. One of Lissa's shoes was found at the beach. Her fingerprints, DNA, and some ice cream were on it." The lawyer raised his eyebrows. "The same kind of ice cream that they found in your freezer at the motel. There was a positive ID by witnesses that it's one of the shoes the girl was wearing that night. She showed them off to the older women when she was talking to them. I hate repeating myself, but you've got to give me some answers."

"I can't explain it," Blass said. "Maybe it came off when she was walking or something. I don't know how my ice cream got on it. I don't know." He pounded his fist on the desk and stood up.

"Get control of yourself, or they'll make me leave," Tyler said, as one of the guards looked harshly at them.

Blass raised his hands in the air, sat down and folded his arms in front of his chest. He glared at the guard and back at his lawyer.

"Explain Lissa's blood smear on your door. Her white blouse, looking like it was cut off her back that the police found under your mattress. Some strands of her hair they found in your tub drain and on your bed. The blood spots they found that were sloppily cleaned up with bleach. The bleach bottles that were stolen earlier from the motel laundry were found under your bathroom sink." The lawyer was frustrated. "There were even traces of the bleach on your hands. That's a lot of damning evidence."

"I told you I can't explain it," Blass said again, trying very hard to keep calm. "I only know I didn't do it. The police planted those things. They must have gone to my room earlier, planted all the evidence, then came back looking for me so they could pin it on me. That's it. They put all that stuff in my room. The motel workers are in on this, and those old bags, too. They've all got it planned out."

"Couldn't have happened. At least, not if you believe John Patel. He said no one other than guests came in or out of the motel grounds from early morning until the police came and asked him to show them your room. And he was there and saw the whole investigation and the processing of everything."

"I don't know how they did it, but I know they did it," Blass said. "They're all in on it. I tell you it's a big conspiracy. To get me. That's it. They're all out to get me. Can't you see that? A coupla' old bags and a freakin' damn foreigner. The police, too. How about you? You in on it, too?"

"Do you hear how crazy you sound?" his lawyer said. "And what were you thinking, running away from them like that? That only makes you look guiltier." Tyler sighed again. Of course he already knew why Blass had run. His client was a wanted man who left all kinds of evidence behind wherever he committed his crimes. This guy didn't have much going for him. The only thing Blass was skilled at was getting out of town without being seen. But that didn't happen this time.

"I ran away because I was scared. I didn't know what they wanted," he said, a tic starting to form in his right eye. Blink, blink, blink. "They were intimidating me. Threatening me. Police brutality. That kind of thing." Blink. Blink. Blink.

"Don't even go there. The motel clerk witnessed the whole thing and his story matches the police report. He's a respected member of this community. And I told you, he's not a foreigner. He's an American citizen. Unfortunately, now that they have you, they've been able to link you to other unsolved murders and disappearances along the east coast. You're in deep water, here. Real deep."

"What are we going to do?" Blass asked. Blink. Blink. Blink. "Better yet. What are you going to do?"

"What's wrong with your eye?"

"Whattya' mean? There's nothin' wrong with my eye."

"All that blinking you're doing. This must have you unnerved."

"You are in on it, aren't you?" Blass said.

His attorney leaned in close to Blass. "Plead insanity. We'll get all kinds of shrinks to testify you didn't know the difference between right and wrong. We'll bring up your sad past again. We'll find as many do-gooders as we can for the jury and, maybe, just maybe, you'll get off again. And, if we're lucky, they'll send you to a mental hospital where you will be treated, miraculously cured and released." He leaned back again. "That's your only chance as I see it. Unless you want to plead guilty and throw yourself on the mercy of the court."

"No to all of that. No way. I'm innocent this time, I tell you. I didn't kill that girl." Blink, blink, blink. "Hey. How about getting me out on bail? Yeah. How about that? That would help."

"Sorry. You're a flight risk. The judge turned you down."

"Well, I didn't do it. And what if I promised not to run?"

Tyler didn't believe him. Ice cream stains and other clues were found at the scenes of five murders or disappearances. Six, if you count Lissa Powell. All the way from Atlantic City, New Jersey, to central Florida. *The police are just too smart. They'll mark Blass's trail and the evidence all the way down the coast. He's going to fry this time.* And, as the father of two teenage daughters, one of whom is a redhead, Tyler didn't want Karl Blass out of jail and at the beaches again.

CHAPTER EIGHT

Next week at the police station . . .

"What do you think?" Officer Lopez asked the others in the room. "Enough circumstantial to get convictions? Even without a couple of the bodies?"

She stood next to a large board covered with photographs, drawings, and outlines of murders up and down the east coast. A map with colored pushpins showed the location of each of the crimes, each pin a different color and each one numbered. Pictures of fresh young teenagers, all murdered or missing, surrounded the evidence. It was a full board.

The other officers nodded their heads or murmured 'yes.'

Jim Hancock, a State Attorney, chewed on his lips. He paced back and forth. He looked at the evidence board, then paced again.

"Let's go over it one more time," Lopez said, pointing as she went. "Stay with me here."

"Number One. Charlotte Levy. Red hair. Green eyes. Fifteen-years-old. Raped and murdered at the beach, Atlantic City, New Jersey. Blass had been seen talking with her at the beach earlier in the day. Her swimming suit cut off her body with scissors which were later retrieved from Blass's home. Ice cream stains and Karl Blass's DNA found on the body. Very sloppy on his part. Went to trial. Blass got off because his attorney cried the blues about his poor abusive childhood and called the DNA questionable. The jury wanted pure evidence like CSI on TV. Case called 'The Beach Boy' Murder.

Number Two. One month later. Linda Nelson. Red Hair. Green eyes. Sixteen-years-old. Raped and murdered on the beach, Virginia Beach, Virginia. Body found at the water's edge. A man fitting Blass's description had been seen talking with her there earlier in the day. Her swim suit had been cut off her body and discarded nearby. Ice cream stains and Karl Blass's DNA found on the body. Sloppy again. Sounds like our boy, but they couldn't find him. He disappeared. Case attributed to 'The Beach Boy.'

Number Three. Ten months later. Carmen Rice. Brown Hair. Brown eyes. Must not have been any redheads around. Seventeen years old. Missing from Sunset Beach, North Carolina. A man fitting Blass's description had been seen talking with her at the beach. No body found. Getting smarter here. Not leaving evidence behind. How'd that happen? Case attributed to 'The Beach Boy.'

Number Four. Two months later, Lula Finch. Brown Hair. Brown eyes. Must like brunettes now. Fifteen years old. Getting a little younger. Missing from Myrtle Beach, South Carolina. A man fitting our guy's description had been seen talking with her by several witnesses on different occasions. No body found. Blass is missing again. Getting smarter. Case attributed to 'The Beach Boy.'

Number Five. Ten months later. Susan Shires, Brown Hair. Green eyes. A mixture of things he likes. Sixteen years old. Body found on the beach in Georgia. He keeps moving south. A man fitting Blass's description seen talking with her in that area earlier in the day. Susan was found raped and murdered. Her swimsuit cut off of her. Blass's DNA and ice cream found on her body. He's stupid again. The case attributed to 'The Beach Boy.'

Number Six. One month later. Lissa Powell. Red Hair. Green eyes. He found another redhead with the green eyes he loves. Seventeen years old. Probably a runaway. Now missing from Palm Bay, Florida. A man claiming to be named Craig Bergen, but really Karl Blass, seen with her earlier in the day. Was supposed to meet her at the ocean at 8:30 that night. Witnesses saw her going to the beach to meet him. No body found. Her blood, hair, and cut-up bloody shirt found at Karl Blass's motel room. One of her shoes, with ice cream stains on it, found at the beach behind The Banana Motel where Blass was living. Same ice cream found in Blass's freezer. Motel clerk saw her go in the room with him. Did not see her come out. Sloppy clean-up job done with bleach at the motel room to eliminate some blood. Bleach found on Blass's hands when we brought him in. He's stupid again. Lots of first-person evidence, but no body found. Case attributed to 'The Beach Boy.' Blass is in custody after trying to escape. Yay for that. A couple of other girls missing up and down the coast. No bodies found. I'm tired of talking. Anybody…"

Lopez opened the discussion to the floor. She leaned back against the wall. "Someone jump in here. Come on. Don't everybody talk at once."

"Is it true you threw him into a thorn bush?" one of the officers said, laughing. Some of the others joined him, chuckling and smiling.

"Negative. You're just jealous because I'm stronger and faster than all of you. Someone else talk," Lopez said. "Make some sense."

"The only thing we're sure of about Lissa Powell is that she was employed for a few weeks at the surf shop," another officer said. "According to her employer, she was an excellent salesperson and dependable. Her fingerprints and DNA were all over her work locker. We ran her prints through the data base again, and nothing turned up. It did match fingerprints found in Blass's room. One of his fingerprints was found in her bloodstain on his motel room door. Her ID looked authentic, but all of it was forged. The best forgeries we've ever seen. Social Security number, everything. I'd love to know who did it. And I aim to find out. It was not done by an amateur. Our investigation showed she was never in any of the area schools. The picture that her employer gave to us was on national television. It wasn't a great picture but showed her fair skin and red hair. We got some leads from that, but they all proved to be dead ends. We couldn't find anyone anywhere who knew her or where she was living. Her address was a vacant lot. That wasn't her home unless she lived in the shrubs with the snakes and the bugs. I personally went to the lot, and after seeing it, find that impossible. We've hit a brick wall."

Lopez was not happy with some of the details. There was a lot about this case she was unhappy with.

"Has anyone contacted the families of these other victims to inform them we have Karl Blass in custody?" Hancock asked. "They'll want to know all about this."

"I can answer that," Officer Clark said. "I called Charlotte Levy's family right away since she was the first of his victims that we know of. Charlotte's mother is still upset that Blass got off for murdering their daughter but seemed relieved that he's behind bars again. She said Charlotte's father was out of town on a fishing trip, but she would call him on his cell phone and let him know what has happened. All of the other families were notified, expressing sentiments similar to the Levy's. They want us to keep them informed on what we know. To a family, they offered to come down here if we need them for anything."

"Good," Hancock said. "What's the latest with the Coast Guard searching the ocean and river? Did they find anything? How about the creeks?"

"Zero," Darrell said. "Neither the coast guard nor its auxiliary have found a thing. No tourist or local have called in a find of the body or anything else related to Lissa. Not a trace of her anywhere on or along the waters. Not in the ocean. Not in the river. Not in the creeks, ponds or lakes. What a shame. We have no clue as to where her body is. I hope a gator didn't get it. And Blass is in denial mode. Still saying he didn't do it so he doesn't know where she is. What a practiced liar. Wants to take a lie detector test for us. Remember, this is the same creep with a history of beating the polygraph. He could have his finger in the pie right in front of you and lie convincingly about it."

Some snickers were heard from the officers.

"Hey, do we know yet who leaked to the press the successful lie detector test that Blass took with his lawyer?" Lopez asked. "The one where he denies killing Lissa."

"No. I didn't recognize the byline," Officer Edwards said. "Nor do we know who managed to get an article in the same paper, right next to the lie detector story, about how Blass has managed to beat the test in the past. Good timing for us, but I'd still like to know who had the savvy to do that."

"I'm just glad he's in lockup now," Hancock said. "He's one of the stupidest criminals I've ever seen. Leaves DNA and evidence galore at all his crimes. He even leaves behind globs of ice cream, his favorite dessert. But, and this is a big one, I've never known anyone who can sneak out of the area as well as he can. He does the crime, then just disappears. And in some cases, so do the bodies. I hope someday he tells us how he manages it." The attorney looked perplexed.

"I just hope we can finally keep him off the street and get justice for these girls and their families," Darrell said. "Before he harms someone else."

"We do have some good news," Lopez said. "I got word today that an anonymous donor has stepped forward and offered to pay all the expenses incurred in the search for Lissa, plus all the trial costs. It's a blank check, folks. The donor will pay for anything and everything related to our work on this case. This unknown person has an agent who says his client is someone who wants to see justice done. Let's hear it for justice." She raised her arm in the air.

First one, then two, then three cheers went up from the officers.

"Fantastic," Hancock said. "That will make our end of it go a lot smoother. And when we're done with Blass here in Florida, all those other states will want a piece of him, too. They're gonna be standing in line with their handcuffs out. By the time everyone has had their go at him, he'll wish the gators got him, too."

CHAPTER NINE

Later in the week . . .

"Yes, a donation to help defray the city and county costs of searching for Lissa and for prosecuting Karl Blass has already been sent to the police. We notified them of the offer, and a partial payment went out this morning. We will pay all of their related expenses as the bills start coming in," Vince said. "One of our Group called the police department and said the donor was a local person. If we have to, we can use the name you gave us."

On the other end of the line, Ginny breathed a sigh of relief. "It was in the newspaper that a benefactor has come forth, and I just wanted to be sure the money was sent. Thank you."

"I think your part is finished for now, Ginny. You performed skillfully in Charlotte's Play. Your presence made everything more believable. Charlotte Levy's parents asked me to pass that on to you. They are appreciative of everything the Cast Members did. It helped them deal with what they went through. There's a sense of peace and justice for all of them now. Thank you."

"Thank you, Daddy. They deserved no less," Ginny said. "And I know they'll do the same for me. For Bobby, when our Play is put on."

"As you know, your Play is the next one we'll run," Daddy said. "It's called Bobby's Play, for your son. You don't have to be a part of this one, but you will be kept informed on what is happening as it unfolds. Unless you want in on it. We'll accommodate you any way we can."

"No, I don't think I could stand being part of Bobby's Play. It would be too painful for me." Ginny said. Tears slid down her lined cheeks. "Do you know for sure when it's going to start?"

"I'll have a Playwright telephone you with the basic details when he has it finished," Daddy said. "You won't get a copy, of course. Only those involved in the execution of the Play will get a copy. But you will know how Bobby's murderer is going to get caught and the outcome. Anything else I can help you with right now?" He felt sorry for her loss.

"No, thank you. I'll wait to hear from you," Ginny said. "I'm kinda worn out from everything. I need some rest."

"Well, if there's anything else you think of, you can call me anytime. You know that," Daddy said. "And thank you for sending another contribution to the Dollar Dreamers. They said it came last week."

"You're welcome," Ginny said. "I'll never miss it. It's money well spent, and I have no one to leave it to now, anyway."

"I'll be in touch," Daddy said.

After hanging up the phone, Ginny began to feel some peace about closure for her son. She went to the wet bar and made herself a stiff drink and sat down in her favorite chair. Though she was wealthy, none of her possessions had much meaning since the loss of her son, until Daddy contacted her, and she was able to put her wealth to good use.

Until Bobby's Play is finished, it is going to be rough. But for Bobby's sake, it'll be worth it. Here's to you, my beloved son. She tipped her highball glass at Bobby's photo and took a swallow.

Ginny kicked off her shoes, sat down in her favorite chair and basked in the moment. *Our turn is coming, Bobby. Your turn.* She took another sip of her drink and thought about how, shortly after Glen Spade got off for murdering her son, she had been recruited for the Theater Group.

Daddy had telephoned her and told her she had been referred to them as a serious enlistee by one of their Recruiters, Theater Group

members who identify potential new members. He had asked her if
she would meet soon with one of their Recruiters to discuss justice
for her son. He cautioned Ginny to tell no one or it would be over.
She would not get a second chance to join. Daddy had explained to
her that the Theater Group is a loosely-knit but fiercely loyal band of
select people, dedicated to hunting down and bringing to justice,
murderers, rapists and other criminals across the country - the ones
who got away or got off. Specifically, he said, they bring justice for
the loved ones of the Theater Group. And they always get their man
or woman. Always.

Ginny remembered how she had been instructed to meet a
private jet at the airport and to be on time. She was whisked off to a
Safe House, one of the private homes where Theater Group members
meet without fear of being watched or recorded. A palazzo along the
Mediterranean was their destination. It was a luncheon date for the
two of them, Ginny and the Recruiter, an articulate, kind man.

One waiter attended to their every need without saying a word.
And the entire tab for the recruitment was picked up by the Theater
Group's Backer. When their meeting was over, she was brought
back to the airport for the flight home.

The Recruiter's instincts had been right. Ginny volunteered
wholeheartedly after their meeting when it was explained to her what
they could do to help her get justice for her murdered son Bobby.

The framework of participants in the Theater Group had been
loosely covered after Ginny became a member. No names were
given for any of them. It was explained that one person is the lone
Agent. He is the one in charge of the whole Group. The agent's
name, Daddy, is used to avoid his real name being known and also to
make it easy for the Cast Members to talk to him on their cell phones
in front of non-members. It appears to others that they are speaking
with a family member when they address him as Daddy.

She learned as the Agent, Daddy knows everyone in the Theater
Group, but the individual Cast Members only know the ones they
must meet in order to get the Play accomplished. The Cast Members
are those people involved in the present Play, the one being the
complete production, written by Theater Group Playwrights, for
bringing the Antagonist bad guy to justice.

"How do they get their information to know how to proceed?"
Ginny had asked. She was told, "Searchers are the ones who work

with the victims' loved ones to get all the information possible about the Antagonist, the crime he committed, his police record, his life history, likes, dislikes, everything. We begin no Play without all of the answers. And, it does not proceed until it is perfect."

Ginny had been pleased to channel her anger and grief into something productive. She enthusiastically offered what she knew about Glen Spade, the murderer of her son. The Searchers then used their contacts and whatever sources needed to fill in the rest. Exhaustive research brought an assurance of success.

The Recruiter had explained to Ginny, who was concerned about how Bobby's Play would be financed, that The Theater Group had Patrons. "These are people who donate cash to the cause," she was told. They don't always participate in the Plays, but they can if they have a loved one in need of justice and want a Play done for them. Any amount, no matter how large or how small, was accepted and given to the Dollar Dreamers. Many of their Patrons were ordinary citizens who had enough of criminals getting away with their crimes.

"Where does the money go?" Ginny had asked.

She had been told that The Dollar Dreamers are Theater Group members who are concerned solely with raising money for the Plays and are responsible for keeping the cash safe and away from prying eyes. American dollars were the only acceptable legal tender. If a Patron wanted to donate foreign currency, the Dollar Dreamers accepted their pledge only after the Patron converted it to American money. No stocks, land or other investments were taken. The Patron had to sell what he wanted to donate and give the cash to the Dollar Dreamers, leaving no trails for others to follow. The Agent audited the Dollar Dreamers' books periodically, and there was always plenty of cash, all of which was used to finance the Plays.

Ginny reflected on the Group and its effect on her emotional well-being. Knowing her son's killer would get what he had coming to him helped ease the anxiety and anger she had been feeling. Today, after the intense emotional and physical investment in Charlotte's Play, she just wanted to rest. She sipped at her drink and then drifted off into a well-deserved nap. She dreamed of her son as a toddler, learning to talk and feed himself. She cried in her sleep as her dream-life went forward to review Bobby's murder.

Later . . .

After Vince finished his conversation as 'Daddy' with Ginny about the money having been given to the police department, he opened a drawer and pulled out a different cell phone, one of many he kept for a short period of time and then discarded. Excited to be making the call, he tapped in Marla's phone number. His pulsed quickened as always, in anticipation of hearing her lovely voice. He shook his head to clear it and center his concentration on matters at hand.

"Hi, Marla, how are you doing?" Vince asked. He got comfortable in his chair.

"I'm great. Getting some rest. How are you?" Marla asked. She absently picked at the band aid covering the area where blood had been taken from her arm to be used in Charlotte's Play. She resisted rubbing the itchy site.

"Good. Where are you at now?"

"Home. I'm going to see Kelly soon. How are things going with the Antagonist?"

"Excellent. Blass is in jail. Evidence is piling up against him, and according to the news, the State's Attorney is promising a swift trial. I'm proud of you and all the other cast members. Your performances were flawless. Charlotte Levy's parents are pleased, too. I hope you got your payment to cover your expenses."

"Yes, I did, thank you. I think I'm getting to that stage, though, where I need to transition to more mature parts. Playing a teenager is getting more difficult for me. I think the clerk at the surf shop was having a problem with my maturity as the17-year-old Lissa."

"Nonetheless, it worked," Vince said. "I think we can switch you into being a 20-something for your next role in Bobby's Play."

"Good. It will feel more natural."

"How much longer will you be a Cast Member for us?" Vince asked. He was hoping she would soon quit acting in that role for the Theater Group and assume a less dangerous position, or his favorite idea, quit the Group altogether.

"I think I'll participate until we have justice for Kelly," Marla said. "Then I'll retire, and we can get on with our lives."

"I like that idea. You know I love you, Marla, and while you're a member of the Theater Group, we cannot further our relationship." He was glad that her role would soon end.

"I know, and I've thought quite a bit about that," Marla said. "But I have to do it for Kelly. Then you and I will have our future together."

"I understand your need to see this through. I'll call you tomorrow. Same time. Same number. Love you, Baby," he said.

"I love you too, Vince."

Marla turned off her cell phone and undressed to take a shower. She washed the still-sensitive areas of her fingertips.

Marla was determined to finish Charlotte's Play, so she toughed it out until Karl Blass was in custody. She was not about to quit on anybody - especially not Kelly.

She finished her shower, got dressed, and prepared to go to her parents' home for a visit with her sister. Marla brushed her short, black hair back away from her face. From her case of many different-colored contact lenses, a clear pair was chosen and inserted in her gold-colored eyes. Checking in the mirror, she liked the natural look her friends and family recognized.

The drive to the home of Marla's parents was short. Marla mused about her romance with Vince. Each of them had felt a spark the moment they laid eyes on the other during her recruitment training to the Theater Group by the Agent, Vince Warren. She thought him to be handsome and thoughtful. He thought she was beautiful and smart.

Vince made an exception for her that he had never done for any of the many recruits he spoke with. He interviewed her personally. That evening, he took her to a romantic dinner, having asked her to not pledge fully to membership in the group until after their date.

The candlelight meal and their sharing of their time together were enough to bond the smitten pair. Vince felt compelled to tell her his story of being kidnapped as a child and the impact the event still has on his life.

Marla's attraction to Vince strengthened, and she opened her heart to him.

Together, they discussed her participation in the Theater Group over breakfast the next morning. Believing in their goals, she joined them.

He was a little disappointed, because one of the strict rules of the group is that none of the Cast Members are to have a romantic relationship with any of the other participants. It keeps potentially complex emotional attachments from affecting the need for strict adherence to the Play. It also diminished the possibility of entanglements becoming toxic for the group.

Marla's commitment to justice for her sister gave her the strength to postpone a further close relationship with Vince until they could be together again. But they spoke to each other on the phone many times during each day. And they met when they could.

Today, Marla's spirits were high. Her active participation in the Theater Group was winding down. It had been an exhausting although rewarding run, but she felt her participation was getting near its end. There was only one more play to go - her biggest role of them all.

CHAPTER TEN

Bobby's Play . . .

Bobby Anderson's murderer, Glen Spade, had been located by the Theater Group during the course of the production of Charlotte's Play. He was found by the Searchers in Tempe, Arizona, where he was working at a construction site. Unskilled and poorly educated, Glen was a go-fer on his job, doing menial tasks such as handing materials to the craftsmen as they worked, and hauling construction trash away from the work area to the dumpster. His pay was low and his crimes continued. Glen had not changed since he murdered Ginny's son.

The appointed Playwright, Nolan Cain, and a Searcher, Marvin Smith, had been taken to Tempe weeks ago on a private jet to finish their assignment. Together, they could share information and tips to assist each of them in the completion of their unique tasks.

Staying at a Safe House afforded the Searcher the freedom and accessibility to perform his duties for the Group without worrying about living arrangements. Throughout their stay, Marvin and Nolan would have no contact with the Host, the owner of the house, who preferred to remain unseen and unknown.

Having already done the background piece, it was time for Marvin to verify what was happening with the antagonist in the present and to research and document Glen Spade's everyday life - where he lives, what he does, whom he sees and knows. Everything possible would be reviewed. The Group would know what he eats and when and where he does it.

The Playwright transferred the Searcher's data into a workable, detailed Script of Three Acts. Although his dedication to the Theater Group was foremost in his life, Nolan was ready to get back to his profession as a novelist. Having joined the Group after his wife Cindy was raped and murdered; Nolan's commitment to bringing criminals to justice has remained a priority for him even after Cindy's Play was completed.

Marvin was recruited for the Group by a member after Marvin's infant daughter, Tara, was murdered. Tara's nanny went to trial but was found not guilty. The nanny's husband admitted to witnessing Tara being abused by his wife, but he fled the country before her trial began. While Marvin's in-home video surveillance showed the woman violently shaking the baby more than once, medical experts disagreed on whether or not those actions had resulted in the brain injuries the child received.

The jury was conflicted, and she was found not guilty. After being released from custody, the nanny boarded a plane for the Far East and, so she thought, out of reach of American justice. She started bragging to close friends that she got away with murder in what she called 'The Filthy American Court.' Tara's Play was carried out in the woman's native country and was one of the Theater Group's greatest successes, given the constraints of working overseas in a different culture.

Marvin relished his work bringing justice to those who had eluded it.

Glen Spade's past was fairly easy for one with Marvin's talents to uncover. Spade was thirty-two years old with an average I.Q. He boasted being a grade-school dropout and reform school graduate. Spade possessed a rap sheet that mirrored his drugs of choice, Opioids. His life revolved around them, and stealing other people's goods supported his habit. Food and everything else followed behind. Spade was a poster child for not legalizing drugs. When he was using, he harmed people and broke laws.

Spade had been treated for Opioid Dependence, with all the typical signs and symptoms. He had a high threshold for drug tolerance and had awakened each day, not to attend work, but to commit petty thievery, house break-ins and muggings with his low-life friends, and all done because when on drugs, committing crimes seemed okay to him. No matter how awful the outcomes of his actions, he rationalized his behaviors. One of his drug sprees led to the murder of Bobby Anderson. All were performed solely for the purpose of obtaining money for morphine, heroin, methadone . . . and so on. He was a drug dealer and a drug user.

"For every Glen Spade we take off the street, plenty more are enticed by drugs to take his place," Marvin said. He sighed heavily and drank the coffee which was brought to him by a server at the Safe House.

"I know, but I still feel empowered each time one of them goes down," Nolan said. "Look at our record. We get them sent to prison which keeps them from hurting more people. I hope Spade is our next takedown."

"Besides drugs, Spade brags about liking cheap blondes and pornographic materials. Nice guy, huh?" Marvin said.

"Your research has been crucial in my writing Bobby's Play," Nolan said. "I finished the final draft early, and it was delivered to Daddy and the Cast Members. Everything has been in the works to do this Play for quite awhile now, so I'll be leaving this afternoon for home. Is there anything else that you need from me before I go?"

"I should be asking you that," Marvin said. "I'm finished, too, and will be on the jet with you. Working here in Tempe was productive, thanks to our host. I was able to get about town, follow the Antagonist, and fill in the blanks of Spade's past and present life without much difficulty. I continue to be surprised how easy surveillance is, given the right tools. All it takes is money and time. And while all that is true, I must admit that I'm wearing out. I'm ready to go home."

Their jobs completed, the Searcher and the Playwright finished their meals, packed their bags and prepared to leave town like all guests do when their time away is over.

Staff carried their luggage to the waiting private jet. The Theater Group members boarded the aircraft and departed for their homes. Cash payments for Nolan's and Marvin's expenses were placed in envelopes for personal delivery when the men got to where they lived.

While they were flying out of Tempe, another jet was bringing Cast Members into the city to begin Bobby's Play.

Aboard the incoming Theater Group jet, Marla Michaels reviewed the Script one more time. She was impressed with its structure and substance, having studied it since the delivery of the final draft.

"This is brilliant. The scriptwriters have outdone themselves," Marla had said to Vince when they discussed it.

She was pleased that Kelly's justice would be served along with Bobby's, during the Play.

After the plane landed, Marla settled into her room and unpacked her suitcases. She rushed through the process so she could make a phone call.

"Hello," Vince said on his end.

"Hi," Marla said. "How are you?"

"Good, Baby. And you?"

"Rejuvenated. I'm here and ready to begin."

"I bet you look beautiful with short blonde hair and blue eyes."

"When I complete my final Theater Group production, I'll do this look for you when we get together," Marla said, giggling. "By the way, how did you like me as a redhead?"

"As a blonde, redhead, brunette, or even if you're gray, I will love you, no matter what."

"I feel the same about you."

"How was your ride to Tempe?" Vince asked.

"Good. Bennie was on my plane, and we had a chance to review the script together."

"Great. The other Cast Members are already in place, waiting to begin. They had their final copy of Bobby's Play delivered, too, so everything is ready to go."

"I'll talk to you soon," Marla said.

"Be safe, Baby," Vince said.

Marla blew a kiss to the phone before she finished.

Vince spoke with others involved in the upcoming production.

"Is everything ready for Bobby's Play?" Vince asked each responsible Cast Member.

"We set everything up months ago and are ready," were their replies.

CHAPTER ELEVEN

Eight p.m. Bobby's Play begins . . .

Benny drove the SUV to the corner a short way from Max's Bar & Grille. As is the policy for all Plays, he stayed inside the vehicle behind darkened windows, so as not to be seen and later identified. As a former Israeli Commando, member of the Shayeter 13, their elite Special Forces unit, Benny understood covert operations into the enemies' territory. The S-13-mandatory twenty months of training prepared him not only for service to his country, but also for the Theater Group.

The passenger's side back door opened and Marla Michaels, costumed as Tina Yarnell, twenty-something hot babe party girl, slid long black-stockinged legs out to the curb. She stood, adjusted her revealing, black leather skirt, and closed the door behind her. Steadied on five-inch stilettos, she got into character and assumed the pose. She stuck out her chest and brushed back her hair like a pro. Daintily, she held her hot red painted nails out in front of her face and gave a half grin of approval.

"Have a safe night," Benny said.

"You, too," Marla said. "I'll be in touch."

She pulled her cell phone off the belt of her over-shirt and punched in familiar numbers.

"Hello, Daddy. I'm here."

"Hi, Baby. Be safe," Vince said. "Call me when you're through."

"I will," she ended the call, comforted by his voice.

Marla hooked the phone back onto the side of her cheap, black belt. She pulled the soft cotton over-shirt down to reveal more cleavage and a black bra, and strutted off into Max's Bar & Grille on dangerously high black heels.

It was dark, hazy, and noisy inside the small bar. She coughed a little from the cigar and cigarette smoke and looked askance at the barstools filled with construction workers downing boilermakers.

Tables and booths held groups having friendly drinks and dinner, but there was no Glen Spade. She spotted the restroom and decided to go there first as that path put her in full view of just about everyone inside Max's. Tonight she wanted to see and be seen. She was confident she would be noticed.

Her spike heels clicked on the tile floor as she confidently strode around the walnut horseshoe bar. She made sure to accentuate her walk, heel to toe, one foot directly in front of the other, as models do, to sway her hips and show off her figure. It was not so easy to do on stilettos. She bluffed her way through it.

The noise of the high heels was like ringing a bell for Pavlov's dogs. Heads turned to see who was clicking in those shoes. Before she got to the restroom door, most of the males in the bar, and some of the females, were watching the beautiful young blonde in the short black skirt. The men watched the new customer out of interest. The women watched out of jealousy, except for one or two of the women who pop in and out of the many bars that line this street, looking for other women. They were interested, too.

Marla pulled a clean paper towel out of the dispenser and, holding it on the door lock for germ protection, turned it to secure the door behind her. She threw that towel into an overflowing bucket that served as the waste can.

She checked her makeup in the mirror and was pleased with what she saw, blonde hair, blue eyes, full pink lips, lots of pancake makeup, with large, heavily outlined eyes. On top of all that, she sported a pair of false eyelashes. The outfit was cheap-looking. It was just what Glen Spade liked, the antithesis of Marla Michaels. She checked deep inside her shoulder bag for the ever-present 22-caliber handgun. It was still there, which added to her confidence. Marla exited the dirty restroom, tossing a paper towel into the trash before the door closed behind her.

Her progress to the bar was monitored by most of the patrons. She claimed an empty stool on the far end, closest to where most of the men were. Hopefully, it would encourage some of them, chiefly Glen if he was on the premises, to approach her to talk. It would prove to be a successful maneuver.

Her well-defined bottom barely touched the red cushion before the bartender informed her that someone wanted to buy her a drink. She turned to identify her benefactor.

"What'll you have?" the bartender asked, eyeing her up and down. "He's paying," he said, shrugging toward a young man chugging a bottle of beer.

"I'll have what he's having," she said to the bartender while smiling at her new friend buying her drinks.

The young man took the cue and, bottle of beer in hand, sauntered her way. As she hoped, he leaned against the end of the bar to talk to her, instead of standing between her and her view of the room.

"What's your name?" he asked, looking her over, head to toe. He chugged some brew and leaned in toward her to listen.

"Tina," she answered. "What's yours?" She looked him over, head to toe, too, and gave him her full attention. *Not bad. Not as good as Vince, but not bad.*

"Jim," the young man said. And off he went, asking her all about herself and then telling her his life's story. If he was telling the truth, something she could never be sure of, he was a single, thirty-five-year old mechanic. But, her experience was that they all claim to be young, single and employed.

Tina gazed upon the nice young man as if there was no one else in the room. It was a skill she had learned from observing successful conversants. However, without being obvious, she was studying Spade's favorite watering hole for Bobby's killer.

One of the lesbians caught Tina's eye. The dark-haired girl in blue jeans and tee shirt raised her glass to Marla and gestured for permission to come speak to her.

Tina smiled, shook her head, and turned away, ending that encounter before it began.

Another hour came and went, along with a parade of men of varying sizes and ages who wanted to make her acquaintance and buy her a drink. She accepted the one bottle of beer only, to avoid anyone slipping something into what she was drinking. When her attention was off the beer, her hand wrapped around the bottle, and she slid her finger into the opening for protection. Although many offers for alcohol were given, Tina sipped from that same bottle.

She was polite, but not overly, to them all, including the older man Jeffrey who approached her wearing a purple, polyester shirt, with dark stains under the armpits, opened too many buttons down. It was not a pretty sight, much like a bad disco movie star. The huge gold colored medallion around his neck and large tattoo of God knows what on his chest did not help. He was a nice person, so she talked with him.

When Jeffrey saw he wasn't really getting anywhere with this one, he moved on to try his charm on some ladies at a table.

The evening and the company were getting old, and Tina was thinking about calling it a night. There was no clock on the wall, so she asked the bartender the time.

"Ten fifteen."

"Thank you," she murmured.

Tina pushed the beer bottle away and shifted her weight to leave. Then the door opened, and three men came into the establishment, strutting their swag as if they owned the place.

Two of the men were identified in the Play as co-workers of the Antagonist. Tina remembered the snapshots and background of each of them that the Searcher had provided for her. The third man, last to enter the building, was Spade, puffing himself up for the females.

Maybe tonight won't be a loss. She sat firmly on the stool again and pulled her beer close.

The group, already sporting a few drinks under their belts, shuffled over to a booth near the bar. They slid onto their seats and ordered some drafts. Though tipsy, they managed to spy the attractive, cheap-looking blonde showing off beautiful legs. When the full glasses were delivered to the table, Glen watched her over the glass's rim as he drank. He was definitely interested.

Tina pretended not to see them, giving her full attention to the latest young man to stop her way. She tilted her head back demurely while talking, to entice her quarry in the booth. Once, she deliberately dropped her purse and bent over to pick it up, showing off her body. She was running out of tricks to pull and hoped that Glen would soon take the bait.

Her posturing worked as, before long, Spade, too, stopped for a chat.

The bartender, Tim, just rolled his eyes at the parade going on before him. He was sure that, on any given night, this loser in particular wouldn't have a chance with her. He watched as Tina spoke to Spade as she did to everyone else. She's one friendly gal.

"What's your name?" Spade said, breath reeking of stale liquor and marijuana.

He was trying to act cool, leaning on the bar and looking her over, then away. A smell of stale beer and sweat wafted her way. Specks of a hastily eaten fast-food dinner flaked across his shirt and pants.

"Tina," she said for the umpteenth time tonight, trying not to be repulsed by Spade's meal on his clothes. "What's yours?" She noticed that his fingernails were long and dirty and his clothes were ill-fitting and wrinkly. She resisted the impulse to lean back and escape unpleasant odors he brought with him.

"Glen Spade," he answered, staring alternately at her face and then her chest. "Want to join us?" he asked, motioning to where his friends were. The two companions in the booth smiled her way. One waved.

"No, thank you," she said politely.

His face registered disappointment.

"But I'll talk to you right here," she said, smiling and fidgeting with her beer bottle.

He turned back and said "Okay." He brightened and got a little closer. More attempts at acting cool. It was really a stretch.

They talked superficially about themselves for the first few minutes. The rest of the evening went according to Bobby's Play.

Spade was pleased with himself and lied all over the place. He told her that he was a former schoolteacher. Lie. Rarely drinks. Lie. Doesn't do drugs. Another lie. And that he was now working as a skilled construction worker. Partial lie.

Oh my gosh. Only a half-lie. She knew that, while he was a construction worker, he was definitely not skilled, unless you count doing drugs and committing criminal activities.

Tina, following his lead and the Play, lied repeatedly, too. She said her name was Tina Yarnell. Lie. She said she was looking for work in Tempe, having recently moved there after her divorce. Two lies. She said she thought he was cute. Big Lie. She completed the lying spree by saying she wouldn't mind seeing him again. Bigger Lie.

Spade said he would like to see her again, too, and that she could trust him. Lie. And that he was just another law-abiding hard-working man, not like one of those creeps she would have to worry about. Lie. Lie.

Tina was surprised they weren't both struck by lightning or turned into pillars of salt for all the untruths flying back and forth between them. She giggled at that thought.

He mistakenly thought she was enjoying his company.

Tina recognized he misunderstood her giggling and giggled some more. She suggested a time and place for them to meet the next night. "I will be at a different bar tomorrow night. At Der Schluss. It's new."

She wrote the name and address down on a scrap of paper for him. He scooped it up, looked at it, and put it in his wrinkled shirt pocket, patting it for effect.

"I want that back," she said, taking back the paper with the address on it. "Just memorize it and be there." She didn't want any loose evidence.

"Are you sure about the address? I thought the bar there was closed," he said, recognizing the street and number. "That's just an empty building now. I remember because we worked on a construction site near there."

"It was," Tina said. "But it's going to be reopened under new management and a new name. Der Schluss. Tomorrow night entrance to the bar will be by invitation only. And I'm inviting you. The general public will not be able to get in. Just friends of the owners. I got an invitation because the owner of the apartment building where I live is also part owner of the bar. He likes me, so he asked me to be there." She crossed her legs to give him an eyeful, thinking maybe it will help him make up his mind.

"Great," Spade said, ogling her limbs. "See you tomorrow night at 9. At Der Schluss." He pronounced it wrong.

"Come by yourself, okay? Cuz your friends won't be able to get in. And, it's Der Schluss," she said, pronouncing it correctly. She batted and lowered her eyelashes." Don't tell your friends about it because the grand opening isn't until the next day," she said, looking over at his companions. There was more eyelash batting. "Anyway, I'd rather it be just the two of us. If you tell them, they're liable to try to get in, and you might get pushed aside. I don't think you'd want that to happen, now, would you? Hmmmmm?"

Eager to please the sexy blonde and wanting to be alone with her, too, Spade agreed. He would tell his friends about Der Schluss after his date.

Tina said she was leaving soon and excused herself to go to the powder room. She did her model walk all the way to the lady's room door. It was an effective strategy.

Spade happily watched her walk away. She looked just as good going as she did coming. He approved. He stayed near her stool for her return and, licking his lips, eyed her half-empty bottle of beer. *Maybe she won't notice if I take a swig.*

The bartender saw Spade looking at Tina's beer and pulled it away from him.

Spade frowned.

Tina waited in a short line for her turn to get inside and pulled out her phone as soon as she locked the door with paper-toweled fingers.

"Hi, Daddy," Marla said quietly, having shed her Tina character.

"Hi, Baby," Vince said. "How's it going? Are you all right?" He held his breath.

"Like clockwork, and yes, I'm fine, thank you. Can you send Benny around to pick me up?"

"Sure can. You ready to go back to the Safe House?"

"Yes. I've got to get out of here and get a bath. Neither this place nor Glen Spade smells very good."

"I'll send Benny right over." He retrieved another phone out of his drawer to make the call.

"Ask him to wait ten minutes, and then he should come pick me up at the end of the block. I don't want anyone from the bar watching me getting into the vehicle," Marla said.

"Okay. Be careful, Baby."

"I will. Talk to you soon."

When she opened the bathroom door, the next person in line thanked her for not taking too long.

"Imagine having only a one-holer for the ladies in this place," the woman said in a husky voice, all the while sucking hard on a cigarette. She blew a smoke ring. The cigarette was burned down to the nub, so she threw it on the floor next to some other extinguished ones and noisily stomped it like one would crunch a cockroach.

The two women waiting behind the smoker agreed with her.

"It's criminal," one of them said nasally. "I have a mind to go and use the men's room." She smiled at her own suggestion and went to the Gents without asking someone to make sure no one was already in there. She wiggled her butt inside and let the men's-room door slam behind her.

Marla nodded her head in agreement with the women and went back to the bar to ask the bartender if she owed him anything. He said no.

Marla motioned for Spade to walk her to the door. In his haste to join her, he tripped but caught himself before he fell. He felt foolish and looked up to see her reaction. She was smiling but resisted making fun of him.

She crooked her finger again and, slowing her pace, was followed by him to the door. She stood and waited for Spade to open it. He didn't get the hint, so she did it herself.

The bartender, seeing what was going on, marveled at Spade's social ineptitude, convinced for sure now that he's going nowhere with this one.

Marla stood outside near the curb and asked Spade to come closer. He moved in and was ready to pucker up.

"It's too bad you don't do stuff," she said, with a shy look, backing away from his pucker.

"What do you mean? What stuff?"

"Der Schluss will be the place to get some good illegal stuff," she said. "I know the new owners very well, and they look the other way for drug dealers and users."

Drugs, his biggest weakness. Blondes, his second weakness. She remembered that from his history.

Spade shrugged his shoulders, but his interest had taken a sharp turn at the mention of drugs. His attention was drawn to his stash.

"What drugs? How cheap? When?" he asked, focused intently for the answer to his dreams of drugs and women.

"They're trying a new strategy to get customers to their opening," Tina said. After saying the words, she realized how stupid it sounded but knew Glen was too stupid to notice. "They'll let you run a tab, pay what you can, and then you can wipe the balance out by working for them if you run out of money. No pressure."

She pulled a cigarette out of her purse and held it in her fingers, allowing him some time to think about it. The cigarette stayed unlit.

Always low on funds and looking for drugs, Spade was hooked. He was mentally doing the calculations of what it might cost him to replenish his stash.

"I'll be there," he said. He took an awkward step toward her, and she backed up.

"Save it for tomorrow night. You'll need all your energy for me then," Tina said. "See you soon, sweetie." She flicked the unlit cigarette out to the street and started to walk toward the corner.

"You bet," he said, eyeing the cigarette for retrieval. He had been hoping for a big kiss but was willing to wait for more. Especially if he was going to score some stuff, too.

Tina turned and smiled broadly, closing the door on the trap laid by the Play.

Spade plucked the unused cigarette off the road and tucked it into his pocket to smoke later.

After his new flame got to the corner, he went back to the bar. He reached into his pocket, brought out a wrapper with some pills in it, and popped one in his mouth. He waited for the bartender to turn his attention elsewhere and snatched Tina's half-empty beer bottle. It provided a warm chaser for the pills. Spade opened the pill wrapper again, counted his stash and was thankful he'd be replenishing his supply soon at Der Schluss. *Whatever that means. Weird name for a booze joint.*

He was feeling good and cheering up. *This is my lucky night.* He rejoined his friends at the table.

None of them believed he would ever be seeing the blonde again.

Before long, Glenn was slurring his speech and feeling drowsy. By the end of the night, he had to be helped out of Max's.

At Papago Park . . .

Rick Cline smoked another cigarette excitedly, leaning back against a park bench while waiting for his contact. He was convinced that, if this works out like he thought it would, he'd deservedly be set for years.

Cline had responded to a flier placed under the windshield wiper of his truck last evening. At the top of the paper was a picture of three young Asian women, scantily dressed and looking submissive. 'Like foreign women and everything your way?' the announcement asked bluntly. 'Then call us now. Don't wait.' There was a phone number in large print on the bottom of the flier.

Cline had looked around the parking lot after taking the notice off his truck window, to see if he was being watched.

The bar had closed, and the grounds around it were bare except for his truck. He hadn't thought to look up at the top of the establishment. If he had, he may have spied the lone, black-clad figure hiding on the flat roof, recording his every move. Cline had dialed the number on the flier and waited for someone to answer.

"Hello, who's this?" a thick voice had said.

"I'm answering a flier," he answered. "It was on my truck windshield. Who's this?"

By the end of the conversation, he had agreed to meet a man, identified only as Cisco, at Papago Park at 8:30 p.m. "Don't be late," the thick voice had said. "Or you'll miss the chance of a lifetime."

Cline was sitting on the bench at Papago Park. *Here I am. I'm all male and ready for anything. Bring it on.*

The simple one or two lines on the flier summed up Rick Cline's lifestyle preferences completely - women and male dominance. He recalled bitterly how he had to flee the area he was last living in to avoid prosecution for his brutal rape and beating of Kelly Michaels. *Why should my life have to be uprooted for doing something like that? I'm the man. She resisted me. What's the problem? I should have killed her when I had the chance.* He regretted how two witnesses had seen him approach the young woman earlier and had seen her rebuffing him before he attacked. He promised himself next time, there would be no witnesses. *I need someone much more subservient and under my control when I want to have my fun.*

He flicked his spent cigarette onto the grass. The opportunity mentioned in the flier might be what he was looking for, a chance for a lifestyle of his choosing without some outside interference. He wondered why it couldn't be like that in the United States.

Cline was still angry that, after the Kelly incident, the police raided his rental unit and took his computer and life's collection of photographs and contacts for women and pornography. It had taken him a long time to amass that enviable collection.

He had thought seriously, after hiding out in various campgrounds and abandoned buildings, of leaving the country and settling in a foreign country. Of interest would be one of those places where men were still in charge, and women and children had to do what was asked of them or else. He was convinced this country here was going downhill because women's rights had ruined everything.

"Cisco here," the thick voice from the phone call said from behind Rick.

"Hey, you scared me, man," a startled Cline said. He turned to see who was sneaking up on him.

"We don't scare men," Cisco said. "But women, now that's another story." He laughed.

"So, what are you selling?" Cline asked, getting right to the point.

"Just what the poster said. We can supply foreign women and a place for them to do what you want, any way you want it."

"Why my windshield?" he asked suspiciously. "You don't know me."

"No, we don't," Cisco said. "But one of our members spotted you talking to an Asian woman at the bar tonight, and you looked like you were in your element. So, we took a chance. Hey, if we were wrong about you, we would have brushed you off when you called. We still can if this doesn't sound like something you want. These numbers are easily changed and replaced," he said, looking at his cell phone. "So, you interested or not? It's your call." He looked tough, bored and about to leave. "Hey, were we wrong about you?"

"I'm interested," Cline said. "But I have to be honest with you, I don't have much money. I mean, I'm willing to pay, I just don't make enough to pay top dollar."

"You're getting in on the ground floor of this new culture, my man. You can run a tab and pay on it as you can. If you can't pay much, you can do some work for us. We always need backup somewhere, sometimes. Right now, the gang needs a driver. Do you have a license?" Cisco asked, knowing that he did.

"Sure, I have a license," Cline said. "I've got a problem, though. I'm sorta wanted by the police. If they stop me for anything and run my driver's license, I'll be extradited out of here."

"What do you mean 'sorta wanted by the police?' Either you are wanted or you aren't." He sneered.

"What I mean is I'm wanted by the police. I'm just sayin'. " Mentioning his police problems made him nervous.

Cisco laughed. "Who isn't, bro? We are all wanted. Everyone in our group is being chased by someone. Don't worry about your license. We got people who make licenses better than the real ones. So, forget it. We'll get you a new one."

"What is this gang anyway?" Cline asked. "I just want to know what I'm getting myself in for." It sounded suspicious, even to him.

"Hey, if you have to ask, maybe we need to walk away from you."

"No, I don't mean anything. I'm just wondering."

"We're a group of men from all over the country who like to have a good time," Cisco said. "American women don't want to do it our way. They're bossy and liberated. They have rights." He frowned at that. "So, we bring in women who'll do what we want. And if they resist, we force them. We use them for whatever we want. We get some for factory workers, and we get some for ourselves. Sometimes we get them for both. We don't have to pay them, and we don't have to keep them. There's always someone who wants to buy what we cast off. We get females from Mexico, South America, Russia, Asia. You name it, we can get it. All ages, all sizes, depending upon what the membership is looking for. We even smuggle them in from places that pride themselves on abusing their own women themselves." He laughed out loud. "Those are our favorites."

"Wow," Cline said. "Love it. This is a real man's biggest dream. Maybe we can make this country great again."

"Hey don't worry about it. The way this country is going, just about anything will be legal soon. We're counting on it. We buy some of the foreign women from their relatives who live here already," Cisco said. "Many of those are thrilled to get some American money in exchange for some worthless female leeching off their family. Getting those types into the country isn't as difficult since their relatives are helping. They do whatever is necessary to bring them in. After a few months, they turn them over to us. If anyone asks about them, the family lists them as runaways. There's no trail to follow."

Cline thought a minute. "What about visas and passports and all of that stuff."

"U.S. visa laws and regulations are complicated, time consuming and constantly changing, so we don't deal with them at all. We're not getting these women to marry, so why do them a favor and get them here legally? We use that as part of our fear campaign against them. We tell them if they don't do what we want, we'll turn them over to the authorities for breaking the law, and they'll get sent back to their county. We break their spirits, and if we have to, we break a bone or two."

"I love it," Cline said. "Sign me up. For whatever I can get."

"First and foremost, you're getting yourself in for a lot of female fun. Your way. Consider this to be your introduction into our gang. Tomorrow night, you get a taste of the wares. Meet me then. Nine o'clock. At the Der Schluss bar. Here's the address. Don't tell anyone about this, or you're out of the fun. Come alone, or we won't let you in. I'll bring a couple of our prize slaves, er, girls, for you to meet. If you work out, I'll take you to one of our, what we call, clubhouses. That's when the real fun begins. Maybe we'll even let you take one home with you to try her out."

"Ain't it grand being a guy?" Rick said. He sat up straighter, full of pride in his manhood.

"You'll appreciate it even more after tomorrow night," Cisco replied. "At Der Schluss, we'll be introducing you to a whole new subculture, right here in the good old USA. Land of the free and home of the brave. Men only, of course."

CHAPTER TWELVE

"If there weren't two witnesses to the crime, I'm sorry, I can't help you," Vince said to someone speaking to him on his cell phone. "Really, I am." He was very uncomfortable. This was one of those difficult times that have happened over the years, where he could not provide justice where it was deserved. It was out of his hands.

"Can't we make an exception just this one time?" Gerry, one of the Searchers, asked. "This crime is perfect for the Theater Group. An elderly couple were out taking their daily, early evening walk, going to get some ice cream. They were accosted by a gang of thugs who had been watching them and casing their retirement community neighborhood. The couple were run down with a car, beaten, and robbed. They even forced the diamond engagement ring off the elderly woman's hand, breaking two fingers in the process. She had a bad heart and died at the scene from a heart attack. The only problem with the whole case is there is just one witness to the crime, Daddy. But he's a good witness. Her husband. He got an up-close look at them and their car. Knows the year, color, make and model. So far, the authorities haven't been able to locate the men or their vehicle. Her husband is desperate for some help."

Vince was saddened. Almost all the requirements for a Play were met. All but one. "The rules of the Group state that there must be two credible witnesses who can place the Antagonists at the scene of the crime. Two credible eye witnesses. It's the only way we can be assured of not bringing an innocent person down. That, and all the research we do prior to executing a Play. I wish I could help you, Gerry. Everything you described makes me angry. These three deserve a Play. I'm sorry we can't do it."

"I understand, but I had to ask. I'll pass it on," Gerry said. "Daddy, the elderly couple in this sad story are my parents." His voice cracked. "We'll bury my mother tomorrow."

Vince heard sniffling. "I'm so sorry, Gerry. Listen. Even though the Theater Group can't take this one on, I'll have someone hand deliver to you the name and number of an individual who will be willing to use his office to investigate this for you and your family. We use this contact a lot in cases we can't do. They're good and not expensive. You can trust them. These murderers will be tracked down, and our contact will get the information to the police. You know it yourself, Gerry. A lot of these criminals think they're too smart to be caught. They believe they know more than anyone else and that they are quicker than everyone else. But with the right resources, anyone, and I mean anyone, can be found. So don't give up hope."

"Thank you," Gerry said. "I'll wait to hear from him."

"And, Gerry," Vince said. "Please accept my condolences for your mother and for what your family is suffering. I'm sorry I can't be at the services, but I'll send someone in my place."

"Thank you." Gerry ended the conversation to go see his father.

Vince put his cell phone down and rubbed his temples. He rubbed his eyes and then down the back of his head to his neck. He picked up another phone and called a trusted Group member whom he knew would attend the funeral for him.

So many unsolved, unanswered crimes. So much injustice, suffering, and hate. We have more than we can handle. Vince resolved to follow through on a Californian's request for a Theater Group chapter on the west coast. He got out his address book and looked for a telephone number.

Later . . .

"Hi, Allen," Vince said. "How are you? And what time is it out there in Los Angeles?"

"I'm fine, Daddy. How are you? It's 8 p.m. I was just finishing dinner," Allen said. He pushed his plate away.

"I'm good," Vince said. "Can you talk privately right now? I have something important I want to discuss with you, and I need your undivided attention."

"Yes. You got it. Barbara's over at her sister's right now. I'm alone, and it's safe." He was hoping this was the good news he had been waiting on.

"It's time we added a west coast chapter to the Theater Group. We're getting overwhelmed and spread thin by having just one Group."

"Too many Plays, too little money?" Allen said.

"The need for Plays, plenty of money," Vince said. "There are many people we want to help and not enough time to do it. We're doing a play in the Midwest right now that could have been handled by a west coast group if we had one. What do you think? Are you ready to go from the job of Solicitor to becoming an Agent? It would mean a drastic change in labor and responsibilities."

"Are you asking me to head up the west coast Theater Group?" Allen asked. "The one you and I had talked about before? Is that what you're asking?" He steadied himself.

"That's what I'm asking. Before you answer, you might want to think it over. It's a big job. When we're running a Play, it's almost a 24-hour-a-day commitment. Can you spare that kind of time and energy?"

"After what happened to Barbara, and the way the Theater Group ran her Play, I would be honored to step up from being one of the Solicitors to becoming an Agent," Allen said. "When do I start?"

"Right now," Vince said. "Get everything in order and clear your calendar, because a private jet will be landing in LA to pick you up and take you to Niagara Falls, New York. I'll let you know exactly when, in a couple days. You and I will meet at a Safe House there to begin laying out plans for the framework of your Group. Just you and I. Together, we'll launch the west coast Theater Group. Understand?"

"I understand," Allen said. He raised his fist and punched the air in response. "This is great news, Daddy. It will be good to see you again. Even though we talk on the phone a lot, I haven't seen you in years. You were just a 20-something when I first met you. You must be in your late thirties now, right?"

"I've definitely aged," Vince said. "I'm looking forward to seeing you, too. Early tomorrow morning, you will be given a folder with all the details about our upcoming meeting. I'm sorry I can't specify the exact date we'll be meeting, because we have something big coming down in another state tonight, and I must be ready for anything. I also thought you would need the extra time to take care of things on your end. I'm sure your law practice will need to be reassigned. I have already found a Solicitor to help with your new Theater Group work, but he will only be temporary until we find someone to replace you. You're on your own with finding someone to take over your law practice."

"I'll be able to meet you whenever you say," Allen said. "I'll need to make some arrangements for Barbara's care, but my daughter can always help out with that."

"How is your lovely wife?" Vince asked. "Is there any improvement?"

Allen's wife, Barbara, had been severely injured more than a year earlier when a drunk driver lost control of his truck, crossed the median and hit her car head on. It was his sixth drunken driving charge in as many months. Despite having lost his license and having served time, he continued driving and drinking, drinking and driving. When he got out of jail and was behind the wheel again, the Theater Group took it on. If the law wouldn't do it, someone else had to stop this irresponsible maniac.

"She's okay. But she still cannot walk without her walker. Her memory is slowly returning and the feeding tube is out," Allen said. "However, the doctors don't believe she will ever be able to dance again. Her ballerina days are over. She hasn't accepted it and cries a lot. So, now she's in therapy and taking antidepressants. And the bills are mounting."

"I'm sorry. I seem to be saying that a lot these days to victims, but I really am sorry."

"We're glad she's still alive, Daddy," Allen said. "That's more than a lot of the Theater Group members can say about their loved ones. Our daughter and I are thankful Barbara is still with us. It could have been worse."

"You're right. Thank God for that. How is your daughter? I forgot to ask about her. The last I heard, she was ready to graduate from college."

"She's great. In her first year of law school now. I'm very proud of her," Allen said. "She's following in her father's footsteps."

"That's good. I'll see you soon. Wait to hear from me," Vince said. "Oh, I want to let you know, both you and I will be searched for bugging or taping devices before we sit down to talk. I know neither of us would intentionally wear any electronics, but they could be planted on us without our knowledge. Just wanted to let you know."

Allen ended his conversation and punched in some numbers on his cell phone.

"It's finally happened. I've been offered the west coast Theater Group Agent's job," Allen said. "I'm to meet with Daddy soon at Niagara Falls. We'll be spending two days discussing the formation of the new group. He's sending a folder of information sometime tomorrow morning by special courier. I'll make some copies and send them on to you as soon as I receive it."

"I'll be looking for it," a woman said. "And it's time for you to dispose of this phone after you hang up."

"Okay," Allen said. "Will we be meeting before I go to the falls?"

"Absolutely. We want to be as prepared as possible on our end. I expect their team will be suspicious and want you searched, so we'll have to have some of our people there to get us the information we want. Keep tomorrow open, and we'll get together."

"Just let me know when and where you want me to be. And, after I meet with Daddy at Niagara Falls, I'll get back to you with a full report."

"Well done," the female said. "We look forward to seeing you tomorrow and hearing from you after you return."

Allen put the cell phone in a bag with some others for destruction. The container was almost full, so he sealed it to be sent out. For just a moment he reflected on his history with the Theater Group and felt some nervous apprehension. Then he put it out of his mind.

CHAPTER THIRTEEN

Der Schluss - 9 pm . . .

From the outside, Der Schluss looked abandoned, but the place was packed with people. Despite the sparse interior decorations, all the booths and tables were full as if it were an operational booze garden. A few beer signs shined from the walls, some of them vintage. Behind the bar, liquor bottles and glassware hugged the shelves.

When patrons entered, they saw the bar filling to capacity with standing room only. They were all there for the duration of the evening. Most of them ordered drinks and meals which came in takeout containers. The barstools were occupied with customers sitting and chatting back and forth or just having bottles of beer. Even though this was the unofficial opening night, the atmosphere was friendly in the manner of a typical local hangout.

The doors were kept locked, and the chosen ones were permitted inside as they arrived.

Spade was proud to be one of the special ones who not only had access to a booth, but also had some free drinks and a beautiful date, Tina Yarnell. He had not told his co-workers at the construction site that he was going there per Tina's instructions for fear of her finding out and dropping him as her date. He planned on telling everyone tomorrow at work, certain it would boost his popularity with the crew, most of whom couldn't stand him. He was aware they thought he was nothing but a dope-head jerk. *When they find out I know of a great place to party and have a hot babe to party with, they'll look at me differently. I'll be respected.* He popped a couple pills which made him feel even better and dreamed about the photos he would take of him and Tina together.

Marla, true to being in character as Tina, had her face covered in lots of makeup. Her short blonde hair was slicked back except for full bangs which fell across her blue eyes, sometimes obscuring them. Every hair was kept in place with heavy professional spray. She was quite a sight.

For the night's special Play, Marla chose a skin-tight low-cut, sleeveless denim top and the shortest, tightest denim skirt she could wear and still be somewhat of a lady. Stilettos with silver-tipped points were her shoe of choice. Silver and turquoise jewelry, lots of it, completed her outfit. She had an unlit hand-rolled cigarette in her hand and waved it around for conversational emphasis and drama.

"You look fantastic," Spade slurred, drinking in what was his idea of a real looker.

"Thank you," Tina said. "You look pretty nice yourself." It was all she could do to get the lie out with some measure of sincerity.

Spade had to agree with her opinion of his look. He was proud of his outfit. He even ironed his clothes for this special night. Wearing blue jeans, western boots, a tee shirt, and topped off with a cowboy hat, he thought he was the picture of cool. The odor of cheap, knock-off men's cologne swirling about him added to the overall effect.

When not ogling his date, Spade was looking about, waiting for the drug connection to approach their booth. No one stopped to talk to them.

Tina found plenty of topics to keep their conversation going as they waited. From drinking and popping pills, Spade was feeling no pain.

"What's the name of this place?" he asked. He was beginning to forget where he was.

"Der Schluss," Tina said.

"What is a Der Schluss?" Spade asked, looking about.

"Just sit back and enjoy. Believe me, you'll never forget it."

All about them, the other patrons seemed to be wrapped up in their own private little parties. There was plenty of drinking and laughing and generally having a good time. Once in awhile someone would get up from their table and talk briefly with someone at the bar or a booth. It was a real friendly crowd. A waiter brought Spade another drink.

"Are you sure he's coming? You know, the drug guy." Spade said. He was almost out of pills and intended to get a super-sized refill. Especially since he could run a tab and, if he couldn't pay it, work it off. What a fantastic deal. It was the kind he had never heard of before and almost too good to be true. He was impressed with being invited on the ground floor of the latest drug dealing policy.

"Don't you worry, he'll be here," Tina said with a wink. "I'll let you know when I spot him." She gave him a big honey-dripped smile.

"Yeah, but maybe he won't get in," Spade said.

"Don't worry, sweetie. They'll let our man in." She winked again. "He's one of the reasons most of these folks are here."

Feeling reassured, he finished his drink and ordered another one. He planned on nursing the next booze along. Already feeling woozy, he was afraid he'd imbibe too much and not be able to score with Tina. For that good time, he wanted to be wide awake and aware of everything. He dreamed of getting a couple pictures of the two of them together so he could show them around at work. For fun, he would post them on the computer, and for drug money, he envisioned selling them.

Country music was playing in the background, interspersed with a smattering of light rock and roll. Occasionally, some of the patrons cheered in recognition of the rockabilly tunes hand-picked for the occasion. It looked like a typical bar, except Glen Spade and Rick Cline were the only ones smoking.

Spade, his cigarette hanging from stained fingers, hadn't noticed that curiosity.

The bartender had observed the two lighting up and pointed it out to one of the bouncers who approached Spade.

"I'm sorry, sir, but you'll have to put that cigarette out," the muscled young man said nicely, but firmly.

"What are you talking about? This is a bar. Everyone smokes in a bar," Spade said, annoyed. He laughed, shooing the bouncer away with his cigarette and making a face as if the guy was an idiot.

"Not tonight, they don't," the bouncer said, taking the cigarette from Spade's mouth. Snuffing it out between his finger and thumb, he gave him one of those 'I dare you to stop me' looks.

"We don't have our fire extinguishers functional yet. Thank you for not smoking," the bouncer announced. He smiled broadly, standing firm. "You and everyone else can light up here tomorrow night to your heart's content."

"Sure," Spade said, not wanting to take on the bigger man. He muttered something under his breath after he thought the bouncer was out of hearing range of his comments.

The bouncer looked back over his shoulder at Spade and glared.

Spade broke from the stare-down and looked away.

Over at his table, Rick Cline cringed when he got his order to put the cigarette out but did what he was told.

"Oh, look," Tina said, as more patrons were escorted through the door. "Here comes our man."

She smiled at her date and pointed to where a tall, muscled, dark-haired man was standing in front of the door.

The object of her attention looked about the room and motioned for a smaller man with long blonde hair, wearing sunglasses, to follow him. Behind the smaller man, another much-larger bodyguard followed closely. All of them behaved like people who are used to being in control.

The two escorts scanned the room while each kept one hand near their waist.

The trio was largely ignored by everyone but Tina who waved their way.

"Tony," Tina said sweetly when the blonde male approached her booth. She stood and gave him a long hug.

The bodyguards were unsmiling, unmoving, and still looking about.

"Tina, my girl," Tony said, after releasing her. "You look good enough to eat."

"Thank you." Then as if an afterthought, she introduced Spade.

"Tony, this is my friend, Glen Spade. You know why he's here and what he wants," she said, patting Spade's arm tenderly.

"Hey," Tony said, nodding his head but not extending his hand to Spade.

Spade put his outstretched hand down and said hello. He was beginning to get bad vibes that he might be in over his head.

Tony and Tina sat down on the same side of the booth, Tony on the outside. The bodyguards stood, one at the end of each bench seat.

No one else in the place seemed to be noticing them.

"Tina tells me you want to make a buy," Tony said, warily eyeing Spade. He reached his hand out and tapped it gently on the table in front of him in rhythm with the music playing overhead. A large diamond ring glistened from his pinky finger, which made a rap, rap, rap sound as Tony kept time with the beat.

"Yep," Spade said. He was beginning to squirm under Tony's hooded gaze and unnerving behavior. Beads of perspiration formed on his forehead. He picked up a napkin and swiped at his face. He crumpled it and attempted to dab at his face again. He regretted doing that in front of them.

"Tina tells me you want to take advantage of our new way of doing business. On the buy-now, pay-as-you-can plan. Just like buying furniture and appliances, only the product's better. Maybe do some work for us if you can't make the payments." His eyes drilled through the weaker Spade's eyes. "This is the thing of the future for our business. Everyone will be doing it soon. Not now, but soon. We're the first. We're always the first." He was not smiling. "And we aim to stay that way."

"Yep," Spade said. He berated himself for drinking too much and for not feeling strong enough to say more.

Tony and his friends were intimidating him into silence.

"I don't know you, so I'm only making this offer because Tina likes you," Tony said. He grinned at Tina and moved closer to her. "And I like Tina." He put his arm around her and kissed her cheek.

She blew a kiss at Spade who smiled weakly in return. He didn't like Tony muscling in on his date.

"Thanks," he said, looking fuzzily around the room for reassurance that others weren't listening to their conversation. He saw no attention focused on them.

Tables and booths were full of patrons busy laughing, ordering drinks, and listening to the music. Everyone appeared to be having a good time. There was good-natured bantering and some were talking in low tones. No one appeared to have taken any notice to Spade, Tina and their tough-looking companions.

"Here's what I'm going to do," Tony said. "My men here will walk with you to your vehicle. No offense, but you look like you could use a little help right now. They'll get your phone number from you, give you some stuff and tell you what you owe us. I'll contact you tomorrow with the payment details. How does that sound? Are you in?"

"Sounds great. Come on, Tina," he said, as he rose swaying from his side of the booth. He was eager to get his stuff and get Tina, too.

The bodyguard at his end of bench took a step back to let Spade stand.

"Tina's staying with me for awhile," Tony said huskily. "She and I got business to discuss." He smiled at her, then shot Spade a look daring him to challenge the arrangement.

"Sure," Spade said, although he was deeply disappointed. Thoughts of the drugs cheered him some. "Call me later, okay?" he said to his date.

"I'll call you tomorrow, and we'll get together then," Tina said. "I'll get your number from Tony." She gave him her best 'come hither' look. "I'll be looking forward to it. It'll be extra special because of the wait. You'll see."

"Good," Spade said, walking away from the booth with a bodyguard on either side of him. He groaned and looked wistfully back at Tony snuggling up to his date.

Tina winked at him and showed some leg. "You take care."

Tony, looking bored, brought his left hand up and studied his fingernails. He put that hand down on Tina's arm as if he owned her.

Once he was outside, Spade's face was numb. He shrugged it off, flush with pleasure that he was going to see Tina tomorrow for some extra special party time, and he was thrilled to be getting some good stuff tonight. What could be better? He marveled how he didn't have to give them any money yet. *I can't believe how good this setup is. He walked toward his van. It's the wave of the future, they said. And I'm in on the ground floor.*

"Which car is yours, my man?" Sammy, one of the bodyguards, asked.

"That van over there," Spade said, waving his fingers wildly about. He was wishing he had a nicer vehicle to impress these guys and Tina, but the van was all he could afford. It looked pretty sad to him tonight.

George, the other bodyguard, shook his head and made a face at the piece of crap Spade was driving. He whispered something to Sammy and they laughed.

The three men stood next to the rusting, faded blue vehicle. Sammy opened the driver's side door, and Spade got in per the bouncer's instruction. He waited for them to speak, hoping they didn't ask him anything, since he was having trouble remembering things.

George leaned against the inside of the open door. He gave Spade a pen and paper to write his phone number on. His hands shook, but he got a blurry set of numbers down. He tucked the pen inside his pocket.

"I want my pen," George said.

It was returned.

"You sure this is your number?" George said.

"Read it back," Spade answered.

George read the scrawled number out loud.

"I think that's it. Yeah, that's probably it. Maybe. Yeah. I think so."

Sammy reached inside his jacket and pulled a plastic bag out of his coat. George did the same. They handed the items to Spade, with Sammy assuring him he would be contacted soon about payment.

Spade leaned over and tucked them into a compartment under the passenger's seat. A big silly grin crossed his face. "This night's looking great. I can't wait to use the stuff you gave me."

The amount looked adequate enough to hold him for awhile. He was sorry that Tina hadn't joined him but didn't feel as if he was in a position to complain about it.

Sammy closed the driver's door by pushing it with his elbow and leaned in close.

"Look, man," Sammy said. "You work with us, and you'll be driving a Ferrari. Understand? Sell some of what you buy. Pay what you can. Work off the rest of your debt, and you'll be on easy street. No more crap van for you, and there'll be lots of Tina's following you home. Got it? You should see the gorgeous babes who chase us around. Not just because we're handsome. They love the money and the stuff we throw their way."

Spade nodded his head and smiled at the thought of being a successful dealer with money and women. He could see himself in a hot car, peddling drugs with a hot blonde. She may even be hotter than Tina. Dreams of the fast life ahead of him clouded the minuscule bit of sense that he possessed.

"Did you have fun at the bar tonight?" George said.

"What's the name of this place again?" Spade asked, slobber running down his chin.

"The Town Hall."

"The Two All?" Spade asked through a foggy mind.

"That's it," George said. "Now get out of here. You'll hear from us later."

Sammy opened the passenger side door, reached in and started the engine.

Spade pulled the shift into gear. The van gave up a cough, bucked, and the rusted vehicle pulled away, lurching down the darkened street.

Sammy and George laughed out loud when the wreck was out of sight. Staying true to the Script, George made a phone call to the police. After finishing his prepared statement, he readied the phone for destruction.

Inside Der Schluss, Rick Cline was in a booth at the other side of the bar. He was deliberately positioned with his back to Marla, in costume as Tina. With the get-up she was wearing, it was unlikely he would recognize her, but she didn't want to take a chance.

Cisco came decked out with an Asian girl on each arm. The dark-haired girls looked to be about sixteen years old and were dressed in revealing outfits. They sat one on each side of Cisco.

Cline was deliberately seated alone on his side of the table.

Cisco wanted to keep him hungry for some female company, to keep his attention.

The taller girl was named Angel, and the other one they called Mita. Both kept their eyes down and spoke only when Cisco asked them a question or said they could speak.

"What do you think of these two?" Cisco asked of Cline. He looked proudly at his girls.

"They're hot," Cline said, licking his lips. He could barely sit still, he was so excited. He wanted a cigarette, but mindful of the 'no smoking' warning, put it out of his thoughts.

"The man said you two were hot," Cisco said nastily to the girls. "What do you say to him?" He glared at them.

"Thank you, sir," each of them said softly. Eyes still downward.

Cisco grabbed Mita's arm tightly until she gasped, his fingers white from the pressure he was applying. "He couldn't hear you," he said. He roughly let go of her arm.

Mita rubbed her reddened arm and said, "Thank you, sir," more loudly.

"Do you girls want something to drink?" Cline asked. "A beer or a mixed drink?"

"Yes, sir," each of them said, eyes still downcast.

"They only drink cheap beer," Cisco said. "They're not worth spending any more money on than that." He reached his arm around Angel and rubbed against her suggestively.

She smiled sweetly in response.

"Good girl. You're learning," Cisco said. He patted her arm.

"I have expectations of my girls," Cisco said to Cline. He gave the two a knowing look. "They must say 'please' and 'thank you,' keep their eyes down unless they are spoken to. And under no circumstances are they to talk unless first spoken to by a man. Especially no stupid female chatting between them. You gotta keep them in their place so they don't go getting uppity or expectin' something. Cuz after they're used, we toss 'em off to someone else."

"That's a problem with some women," Cline said. "They yak, yak, yak. You can't shut them up. It's better to train them right from the start, so they know how a woman should behave." He was really getting into it. "I wish females here in the US were trained better. They think they can run things."

The bartender brought each of the girls a bottle of beer, and they kept their eyes down and said their 'thank you's' in voices just loud enough to be heard. He seemed not to notice their discomfort.

"Those are good rules you have," Cline said. "Otherwise, they might need to be taught a lesson." He was feeling powerful from his own domineering speech and observing Cisco with the vulnerable teens. He wished Cisco would let one of them sit next to him. He'd like to have them both but would settle for just one to slap around.

"I like the way you think," Cisco said. "Machismo. Very important. How about you, Mita. Do you like the way our man here thinks?"

"Yes, sir," Mita said with a half-smile.

Cisco rubbed Mita's slim, bare thigh with his hand.

She smiled weakly and said, "I like that."

"Good girl," he said.

Cline could hardly stand it anymore. Cisco was getting all the action and he wanted some for himself. *When is my party going to start?*

"You want to go sit with him?" Cisco said to Mita. "Huh?"

"Yes, sir," Mita said. She started to get up.

Cisco slapped her face.

Cline looked anxiously around, but no one seemed to be noticing what was happening in their booth. Either they weren't watching or they didn't care. Maybe both.

"I didn't tell you that you could go yet, did I?" Cisco asked Mita nastily.

"No, sir," Mita said with tears in her eyes. She brushed dark hair away from her face and kept her eyes downcast.

"Now you must be with me tonight," Cisco said. "You still have more to learn. And you know what that means."

"Yes, sir," Mita said, not looking at him.

"How about Angel?" Cline said. "She could come sit with me. Mita can take her turn later."

Cisco was about to answer when the bartender made an announcement.

"Sorry folks, we'll have to shut down early tonight. As you can see by our unfinished décor, we still have a lot to do for our Super Grand Opening tomorrow. We look forward to seeing all of you when we officially become the best bar in town. This place will look great and will be rockin'. You'll want to be here for our grand prize drawing tomorrow night. And remember, drinks will be half price from two to four pm. My thanks to all of you for coming tonight. Our ushers will now see you out."

With that proclamation, four burly bouncers started directing the customers to the door. Motions were made for everyone to leave.

The patrons started getting up from their tables and booths without protesting. They put tips down for the waiter and bartender and grabbed their bottles of beer for a last swallow. Some of them murmured to the others that they would see them tomorrow. A couple of them embraced.

One of the bouncers stopped at Cline's booth and pointed to the door. He stepped back to let them get out.

"Angel," Cisco said, getting up from his seat. "You will go with Cline tonight."

Angel nodded her head in agreement. She managed a half-smile.

"How is that for good faith?" Cisco said. "You haven't given us any money, and already you've made a contact with one of our special girls." He smiled. "The others we have are prettier than her," he said. "But she will do for you for now."

"Fantastic," Cline said in anticipation of the private time he would have all night with the lovely young Angel. She was more than pretty enough for him. He was already envisioning dominance his way. His pulse fluttered in delight.

"I will telephone you tomorrow to discuss how and when you will pay for being in our group. You will find our conditions to be very affordable." He smiled, showcasing a gold grille covering his teeth. Cisco grasped Mita tightly by the arm and pulled her close.

Cline wrote his telephone number down on a card and passed it across the table.

Cisco grabbed it and put it in his shirt pocket. "You stay here," he said to Mita. I'm gonna walk these two to his car." He turned and pointed his finger inches from her face. "Don't move or leave your seat, or I'll deal with you later."

Mita nodded her head in agreement without looking at him. "Yes, Sir."

Cline got up from the booth, cocked his head to the door, and took Angel by the arm. She submissively followed alongside him. He wanted to hit her now just because he could but decided to do it later when he was alone and could enjoy her fear and crying for him to stop.

Der Schluss emptied within minutes. The customers walked to their cars, some stopping to light cigarettes, others talking in small groups. The bar's door was locked when the last customer exited, and the lights were turned off. None of the patrons left the parking lot although some were in cars with the engines idling as if ready to go.

Cline, Cisco, and Angel walked to Rick's truck.

Cisco grabbed Angel's face with his left hand and, squeezing it, brought it up close to his. "You be good to him. Understand? I don't want to get any bad reports." He kissed her nose.

"Yes, Sir," Angel said. "Thank you. I liked that." She smiled nervously and pushed wisps of dark hair from her pretty face.

"They're just like dogs," Cisco said. "You gotta show some muscle to keep them in line. If they don't listen, you kick them around and don't feed them." He laughed out loud. "And if they do listen, you give them a small reward. One that you benefit from, too. It's all about the men."

"You got that right," Cline said with a big grin.

"She's yours for the night," Cisco said, smiling. "Enjoy."

"Don't you worry. I will," Cline said. "And she will, too."

Angel opened the truck's passenger door and slid in. She stared straight ahead so as not to anger her new captor and risk getting struck.

Cline got in the driver's side, closed the door, and rolled down the window.

"I'll telephone you tomorrow morning, and we'll finish the details," Cisco said, pulling a self-rolled cigarette from his pocket. He lit the short tobacco stick and inhaled deeply. "I needed this," he said, blowing smoke into the air. "Imagine not being able to smoke in a bar. Ridiculous."

"I'll wait to hear from you," Cline said. He started the engine and pulled away from the parking lot, the blood surging through his veins in anticipation of the good times to come.

When Cline's truck was out of sight, Cisco put out his cigarette and tucked the butt into his pocket. He pulled out a cell phone and hastily made a call to the police, reciting his speech according to the Play.

The engines of the vehicles in the parking lot were turned off. The Der Schluss customers started to walk back inside, murmuring congratulations to each other for a job well done.

Cisco prepared his cell phone for disposal.

"Act Two is over and done, everybody. Great job," the bartender said aloud when they were all inside. He was high-fiving those closest to him.

Cisco turned to Mita and asked, "Are you okay, honey? I didn't hit you too hard, did I?" He touched her cheek then hugged her.

"I'm fine. I made it look worse than it was," Mita said, laughing. "I hope Bo-Bae's all right."

"She's smart and knows how to handle herself," Cisco said. "And she and Cline should be intercepted before too long. She's going to call Daddy after they get stopped. Daddy'll call me, and we can pass the word around so everyone knows she got out all right." He called out to the Cast Members, "Now let's get this place put back the way it was, people, and we can all go home."

Immediately, all around him, willing hands were busy packing up everything brought in. Liquor, glassware, and snack items were put in boxes and placed outside in waiting trucks. Cases of beer and empty bottles were stacked neatly for loading. Garbage bags with the night's refuse of catered food containers, napkins, and other trash were removed and carried out for placement in Sammy's van. Cast members monitored the cleanup.

Marla came out of the bathroom wearing sweatpants and a tee shirt, looking nothing like the pretend Tina she had been earlier. She had taken off the stilettos and replaced them with sneakers so she could help with the cleanup.

Tony hugged her and told her what a great job she did. "I'm so proud of you."

"I hope we got those cigarettes out in time," Sammy said. "Hey. Can anyone smell smoke or tobacco in here?" He tilted his head back and started sniffing the air. "If the police come around, I don't want them getting a whiff of that. And how about that cheap cologne Spade was wearing. Anyone smell it now?"

They all agreed the odor was gone.

"There's just a faint smokey smell," George said. "Let's open the back doors to air this place out. By the way, my thanks to all you ladies and gentlemen for not wearing perfume and cologne." The Cast murmured appropriate replies. "And don't forget to double and triple check what each other has done to clean this joint up."

"What about this?" Marla asked, holding up a chipped enamel bucket full of old, stale cigarette butts she found under the bar. "Do you want to toss this, too?"

"No, put that back," Sammy said. "It was there when we got here. Probably from when the place was operating as a bar. It might pass as the source of the tobacco smell if the police get a whiff and start looking for it."

Marla put the container back where she found it.

Some of the workers pushed wide the doors of the two back exits. A couple of them went out to the parking lot, looking for anything the Cast Members may have dropped.

The others bustled about to finish erasing the evidence of their evening. Tables and chairs were put back the way they were before the doors had opened this evening. Most of the light bulbs were removed, and the paper towels and toilet paper were taken out of the restrooms. A crew of the Cast, carrying the damp rags the bartender had used, hustled about, wiping down every surface area that may have been touched during the Play.

Finally, when the place was restored and cleared of Cast Members, Sammy, starting at the front door, spread dust from a cloth sack. He put the dust particles in a sifter and went from the front of the building to the back, moving the sifter back and forth in an effort to obliterate footprints and make the place look as if it hadn't been occupied in months. He was skillful, taking care not to put too much around so it looked staged, but just enough to appear natural. He threw some up on the ceiling fans and light fixtures. Sammy backed his way out the door, finishing the job.

When the Cast finished and closed and locked the back doors behind them, they were all reminded to empty their pockets of anything connected to the night's Play. Those items were tossed in trash bags for incinerating.

The bouncers took one last look around and gave the order for everyone to leave the property. Vehicles slowly, methodically, pulled away from their spots. The caravan gained speed and the cars started, one at a time, to take different side roads, until the group had dispersed, and the procession was no more.

One lone figure remained to brush debris and stones where tires had disturbed the grounds outside the building. Job finished and broom in hand, the last of the Cast wandered off into the darkness.

CHAPTER FOURTEEN

Glen Spade cruised his van through the winding streets of the city, weaving back and forth across the line. Thoughts of the drug-filled days to come were on his mind. Rock tunes blared from his favorite radio station.

Impaired from drugs and alcohol, his knowledge of back streets and alleyways was no longer available. He was pleased with his new drug contacts and excited at the anticipation of seeing Tina tomorrow. His mind was concocting ways of having his fun with her. The music was loud, and if it weren't for the flashing red lights in his rear view mirror, he would not have noticed the police cars closing in on him. He regretted having swallowed the pills he had in his special stash.

"What's up, officer?" Spade asked out the rolled down window. "Somethin' wrong?"

"Your tail-lights are out," Officer Johns said. "Please get your owners card, drivers license, and insurance papers and hand them to me."

"What do you mean, my tail-lights are out?" Spade said. "You're crazy. They work perfectly fine." He was surprised. "I know they are because I just had the van inspected."

"Well, they're not working now. Step out of your vehicle and show me your paperwork," Johns said more forcefully.

He motioned for two other officers who were shining their lights into the van's back windows to join him. They came and stood next to Johns.

Empty-handed, Spade opened the door and missed the step. He fell down, looked from one officer to the other, stood up and shifted his gaze nervously to the interior of his van.

Two officers stayed close by. They instructed Spade to put his hands on the side of the vehicle, spread his legs wide, and one of them patted him down.

"You don't have any needles or anything on you, do you? I'm not gonna get stuck when I check your pockets. Right?"

"Nah," Spade said.

He was clean.

"I'll show you my lights are fine," he said.

"Ok, let's take a look," one of the officers said.

Spade staggered to the back of his vehicle. "You're making asses out of yourselves," he slurred. "Good grief."

An officer shined his light on the broken plastic covers and bulbs, all cracked and darkened.

"I just had this van in the garage to the tune of lotsa' dollars," Spade said. "That musta' happened back at the bar." He shrugged his shoulders. "You can't fine me for something I don't know nothin' about. I'm leaving." He staggered toward the front of his van.

"You're not going anywhere yet. Where's your driver's license, owner's card and insurance papers?" Johns said again.

Spade started to sweat. "I left them at home. They're not here." He fidgeted, looking nervously at the van. He leaned into the door to steady himself.

"You left all of your paperwork at home," Johns repeated. "Everything?"

"Yep. I can go get it and bring it down to the station." He was looking guilty but hoping for a break. "Yeah, that's a good idea. I'll go get it."

"I don't think so," the officer said. "You don't look fit enough to drive. Have you been drinking?"

"Just one. Back there at the bar," Spade said.

"What bar?" Johns asked.

"I dunno. The Call or the Hall or somethin' like that."

"We got a tip that a vehicle with this description had just made a drug deal in a parking lot. Do you have any drugs or weapons on you or in your van?"

"No. I don't do drugs, and I don't carry weapons," Spade said, trying to lie convincingly. He smiled crookedly, certain he was smarter than the officers.

"Sit down here before you fall down again," Johns said. "May we search your van?"

"Sure." Uncertain of whether he had drugs or not, he was still feeling secure.

Johns decided to try something. "Where would the drugs be hidden, if you have any?" He gave Spade his most sincere look.

"Somewhere under the passenger's seat," Spade revealed. "But I don't think they're there. Look for yourself." His eyes enlarged when the drug-sniffing dog was brought out of the police car.

Johns stood next to the seated Spade while Officer Conrad handled the dog. The search started on the passenger's side of the van. The yellow lab lowered his head and sniffed the seams of the vehicle. His canine brain was associating the odor of drugs as if it were his toy, and his respirations intensified as familiar, rewarding smells were recognized. Fully engaged in the scent, the lab abruptly sat and stared at the passenger side door. Conrad gave the dog a treat and began to play with him. He took the dog aside and showered him with affection.

"I thought you said you have no drugs," Johns said to Spade. "The dog's behavior tells us otherwise. You can cooperate with us, and we will try to work with you or you can continue to pretend there's nothing there, and we will promise nothing. What will it be? Will you cooperate?"

Spade struggled to remember whether he had drugs or not. He didn't think he did, but opted to cooperate and see what happened. His judgment impaired, he figured he might be able to go home rather than spend the night in jail. That would give him plenty of opportunity to pack up and leave town.

"If I have any they might be under the seat," he offered. "In some bags."

"What's under the seat?" Johns said.

"My stash. Just some pills, that's all. It's stuff I use. I don't sell or nothin'. "

"How about weapons. You packing? Any needles under the seat? We don't want to be surprised by anything. Tell us now."

"No. I never carry weapons on me. I don't like them things." He was glad his Walther P99 was well hidden at his house.

Johns did the Miranda piece with Spade, who grunted that he understood his rights.

"Check under the passenger's seat," Johns called out to the other policemen.

While they went to the other side of the van, Johns gave Spade a sobriety test which he failed.

"If you woulda told me I was gonna have to do this, I'da practiced," Spade said. "It's your fault I flunked. I'm gonna tell the judge all this, too."

"Can I quote you on that?" Johns said. "Verbatim?"

Officer Thomas used the lever and pushed the passenger's side seat all the way back but couldn't see anything.

"Where under the seat?" he asked. "Exactly where are they?"

"Pull up the mat. There's a compartment under it," Spade said. He began to wonder whether or not he was supposed to tell them that. "Will this make me lose my new drug connection? I need those pills."

"Can I quote you on that, too?" Johns asked.

Spade, proud of the officer wanting to quote him said, "Sure. I got lots more you can quote, too. Quote this." He made a rude gesture.

Thomas lifted the mat to find a crudely cut lid. He used a screwdriver lying under the seat to pry off the top. Tucked inside were two plastic bags full of pills. He took them out and held them up. "These for a medical condition or recreation?" he asked Spade.

"Come on. Do I look like I have a medical condition? I'm in my prime. I got swag." Spade said, puffing out his chest. "Like I said. It's just stuff for my use. I don't deal or nothin'. I don't even know why I'm talkin' to you. Do you think I'm sayin' too much? Could it be the drugs I took earlier? Somethin' doesn't sound right when I say it. I don't understand myself. Am I making sense to you?"

"Could you repeat all that? Johns said.

"No."

Thomas tagged and bagged the evidence.

"You have any more of that stuff hidden anywhere else in the van?" Johns asked. "Or anything else you shouldn't have or maybe something you haven't told us about?"

"Nah." He was starting to get upset when he remembered something. "Hey," he said to Johns. "You said you got a telephone call about a drug deal. Who tipped you off? I want their name and number. I wanna pay them back. I'm not gonna do anything bad or anything. Oh, my God, did I just say that?"

"It was an anonymous call. Untraceable," Johns said. "But it looks like our source was a good one."

Spade cursed whoever narced on him.

Thomas finished with the pills, went to the back of the van and opened the doors. "Are we going to find anything here?" he yelled. "Last chance. Tell me now."

"No. Nothin' else." He was relieved that the pills were the only illegal items he had in the vehicle. "At least I don't think so. I'm not sure. Look to make sure. Okay? Tell me if you find somethin'. What did I just say?"

The officers passed questioning looks back and forth amongst themselves.

"If you say so," Thomas said. "But we're going to look, with your permission."

"I say so, so go ahead and look all you want. Geesh," Spade said cockily. "Go ahead. Knock yourself out. Have fun. I'm not worried. Should I be worried?"

The policeman began to move some items around in the back, behind the seats. It was fairly well kept, clean and orderly. A fabric bag of tools was opened with nothing out of the ordinary found. The police opened a box of incidental items including a flashlight, bungee cords and some more tools. The last thing in sight was a white plastic bag tied at the top.

"What's in this plastic bag back here?" Thomas said.

"What plastic bag?" Spade asked. "I don't have anything like that back there." He started to move toward the back.

"Stay right where you are," Johns said. "Now, are you going to tell us what's in there or do we have to find out for ourselves?"

"I'm tellin' you, I don't have a white plastic bag. It's not mine. At least I don't think I do. If there's a plastic bag there then you put it there. Yeah. That's it. You put it there."

"We gave you a chance," Johns said. "Open it up," he yelled to the others.

Thomas untied the knot in the bag and spread it wide open. He saw a couple of gray sweatshirts folded neatly on top.

"There's some sweatshirts in here," Thomas said.

"They're for my work. And they were in a cardboard box, not in a plastic bag. What are you trying to pull? Boy, if you're taping this, you're in big trouble. I better not see this on one of those TV cop shows. I'll sue all of you. Hey, will I be on TV?"

"All I'm doing is going through your things, with your cooperation. Now, what do we have here?" Thomas said, pulling two items from the bottom of the bag. The first one was a clear bag of leaves. "Cannabis, I'll bet," he said aloud for the others to hear. "And a plastic-wrapped brick of something. And, whoa. What's this?" he said, pulling a handgun from the bottom of the bag. "I thought you said you didn't have a weapon."

Thomas walked around to the side of the van where Johns had handcuffed Spade.

"Do you have a permit to carry a concealed weapon?" Thomas asked, holding up the Walther P99 for them to see.

"No. Hey. How'd that get there? That's not my gun. I don't own any weapons. Where'd you get that? That was at my house. What's it doin' here?"

"It was in this bag under your sweatshirts. You must have forgotten you transferred it from your house to here. You seem to be forgetting a lot of things we found here," he answered, holding up the white plastic bag.

He placed the gun back in the bag. "I suppose these items aren't yours either, then," Thomas said, pulling out the clear plastic bag of leaves and a purple-colored brick-shaped package.

"Looks like about 24 pounds of cannabis and a kilo of cocaine," Johns said. Alarmed at the findings, he called out to Conrad to place the dog in the car and join them.

"Check for priors on this guy and run the license of this van," Johns said to his fellow officer.

"Johns is right, isn't he? Cannabis and cocaine," Thomas said to Spade.

"I don't know what you're talking about. They're not mine, either," Spade said. "What's going on here? Where'd you find that stuff?" His eyes frantically darted from one officer to another as his head cleared a little to the realization of the predicament he was in.

"What are you guys tryin' to pull? You went to my house and got that stuff, didn't you? Look, I'm tellin' you straight. Those drugs were stored at home for a couple of friends. How'd they get here along with my gun?"

"You had this at your house?" Thomas asked. "Who'd you buy it from?"

"I bought the pills from some guys at a bar," Spade said. He didn't want to reveal which bar in case he needed more stuff later. He couldn't remember the name, anyway. "They had a new program where I could take the pills with me and pay on tick. If I couldn't pay, I could work off my debt."

The officers just stared at him. They were momentarily speechless, and it was all they could do to keep from laughing. They couldn't believe the crazy story he had concocted. Everyone knows that drug dealers get their money up front. They never let you work it off. It's cash or else. The policemen looked at each other for the stupidity of this guy thinking they'd fall for a story like that.

"So you're telling us that the bad guys who sell drugs, the guys who always want their money up front, the guys who would break your legs and shoot your mother in front of you for nonpayment, are letting you buy on credit, and then you can work it off later?" one of the officers said.

"Sure, I'm tellin' you that. That's what they told me. My God, don't you see the potential in the market for that?" Spade was all pleased with himself. "I guess I knew something you guys didn't know, right? Hah."

"I guess so," Johns said. "But, we're gonna have to take you in tonight." He walked his prisoner to a police car.

"You've got quite a record," Conrad said when he saw them coming. "Did some time for possession. Possession with intent to sell. Petty theft. Armed robbery. And the big one - up for trial but acquitted on a murder charge."

"I was cleared on the murder charge."

"You were acquitted," Conrad said. "The witnesses refused to testify. There's a difference."

"Not to me. Ain't America grand? I'm free and doing just fine, thank you."

"Not for long," Johns said, helping his prisoner into the back of the car.

CHAPTER FIFTEEN

Angel squirmed uncomfortably in the passenger's seat of Cline's truck. They had already gone several miles since leaving Der Schluss, and she was beginning to feel uneasy in the company of a foul man like him. She couldn't turn around to see if anyone was tailing them for fear of his striking her, so she kept her eyes down. She hoped she didn't have to pull her weapon.

"I can't wait any longer, Angel," Cline said, pulling the vehicle into a dead end alley. He shut off the engine and leaned toward her, confident the darkness from tall buildings on both sides would keep them from being seen.

"Yes, Sir," Angel said, panicking at the thought of his touch.

Out of the corner of her eyes, she could see that they were alone at the dead-end street with no exit. It was blocked on the front and both sides by dated, run-down industrial buildings. If she got out of the vehicle and ran, she would have to run toward the back of the truck. Her mind was racing with thoughts of how to get away and quickly access her gun if needed.

"Get out of the truck now," Cline instructed.

"Yes, Sir." She managed a fake smile. She was mustering the courage to pull her gun from her skirt lining. Her hand clutched the bulge where the pistol was hidden.

"And stop saying 'Yes, Sir,' Cline said. "I want you to say my full name and tell me you love me and that you like everything I do," he ordered. "Do you understand?" He had a tight hold on a chunk of her hair.

"Yes, Rick Cline. I understand. And I love you and like everything you've done so far," Angel said, wanting to be as cooperative as possible without jeopardizing her life or physical well-being.

"Good girl," Cline said. "Now get out." He released his grip, half pushing her toward the door.

He slid across the seat to her side, reached across the frightened girl, and opened her door. He patted her bottom when she got out of the truck and slid out behind her.

It took all she had not to slug him when he touched her.

"You didn't say you liked that," he said nastily. His eyes narrowed, and he raised his hand as if to strike her.

"I liked it when you touched me, Rick Cline," Angel said as convincingly as possible. She felt like vomiting.

"Good." He pushed her back against the open truck door.

From behind the vehicle, a spotlight shined on a surprised Cline as he was trying to undo his zipper.

"What's going on here?" a voice called out. The light moved closer to the truck.

"Nothing," Cline said. "My wife and I were just going to have a little fun, that's all. You had better not say anything," he hissed into Angel's ear. He squeezed her slim arm tightly and pulled her behind him, closer to the truck. Rick let go of the girl and took a couple steps toward the light. His attention was riveted on learning who was interrupting his fun.

According to the Play, Angel slowly slid the gun from her skirt to the floor of his truck. When they found it, it would be traced back to a private owner from whom it had been stolen.

"Help. Somebody, help me," Angel called out. "This man has kidnapped me. I'm being held prisoner." She stepped forward and kneed Cline in the groin, causing the surprised man to bend down and grab himself. She ran toward the source of the light, sobbing and crying for help.

Cline stayed crouched down, his pants having fallen to his ankles. Bent over in pain, he held his genital area with one hand and grabbed at his pants with the other. The discomfort and shock of what had happened rendered him speechless.

"This is the Arizona State Police. Don't move," a man's voice called out.

Still agonizing over the crotch kick, Cline tried to pull at his pants.

"I said don't move," the policeman said, gun drawn and moving in to handcuff him.

Another policeman held his taser at the ready .

A policewoman covered Angel's shoulders with her jacket and led the crying young woman to the police car.

Between sobs, Angel repeatedly said, "Thank you, thank you. I was so scared. He hit me and tried to rape me. I'm not his wife. He bought me from another man. I'm not even an American. They kidnapped me from my home in Seoul, Korea." In keeping to the Play, she skillfully recited her lines.

"What?" Cline said. "That bitch is lying. Wait 'til I get my hands on you," he called out to the tearful teenager.

Angel, sobbing and shaking, cowered in fear behind the policewoman. "I need to sit down."

The policewoman glared at Cline. "If what she says is true, you'll not be touching another female for a long time," the officer said. "Get used to it."

By the time the police finished their investigation, Rick Cline was being held for human trafficking, assault and battery, and attempted rape. They found the gun in his truck, which proved to be stolen. Upon searching his home, they uncovered pornographic pictures of Asian children on his computer and in his bedroom. That added possession of child pornography to his list of charges. Cline denied it all.

Angel proved to be a good witness, providing the police with information on the brokers who kidnapped and smuggled her and other young girls into the United States from many countries.

"My real name is Bo-Bae, not Angel. My family lives in Seoul, South Korea. I was kidnapped and placed in a criminal network that arranged labor for me and other girls. We were forced to work at places like massage-parlor-brothels operated by the traffickers."

Angel testified how her debts mounted as she was charged thousands of dollars for repayment of getting into the country, taxi services, food and shelter. The exorbitant costs kept her in debt which she could not pay off from the tips she received from customers. She testified to a combination of severe physical and psychological abuse that was used by the traffickers to keep her and the other victims from contacting the authorities once they were here.

Cline tried to explain away his actions to the police, claiming he was just spending the night with a girl he picked up at a new bar. He told them about Cisco, and how he met him at Der Schluss for drinks with Angel and Mita. He claimed Angel went with him voluntarily for a night of fun, nothing else.

Angel denied his story.

Days later . . .

The police went to the address Rick Cline gave for the bar. When they pulled into the parking lot, the officers were skeptical.

"This doesn't look like it's been used for a long time," Michael, one of the policemen, said. "The owners told us it's not been rented for almost a year. And they claimed on the night in question, they had cruised by here to see if everything was all right and there was nothing going on and no one was around."

"It's early in the day yet, and we have the right paperwork so we might as well go in," his partner Joel said. He opened the car door and pulled keys from his pocket that the owners had given him.

Stepping inside the vacant building, Joel started taking pictures.

"Look at all the dust," Michael said. He sneezed and waved his hand to disperse dirt floating in the stale air.

As the officers moved about kicking up more particles, Michael sneezed again. "Allergies," he said.

"It's the police. Anyone here?" Joel called out.

No response.

The officers walked around the bar, opening doors and peering into cabinets and drawers. Nothing. Cautiously, they went to the hallway and looked in the bathrooms. Rust rings circled the dry empty toilet bowls. Dirty sink spigots corroded in odd-angled, fixed positions.

"There's no way this could have been opened as a bar that night," Michael said. "Look at the condition of this place."

Joel sniffed the air. "Do you smell something?" he asked as they moved back into the bar area. "Like stale cigarette smoke?"

"I can't smell a thing," Michael said. "The dust is too strong, and my allergies are acting up." He sneezed again and wiped his nose. He looked down at their tracks on the floor and blew his nose again. "Allergies."

"Maybe I'm wrong," Joel said. "Wait a minute." He pulled a small bucket of old cigarette butts out from under the bar. A spider web was spun over the opening. "Here's the source of that smell," he said, showing it to Michael.

The officers completed their search of the building and finished up in the parking lot. They had found nothing of importance. When the dumpster out back was opened, an empty container yawned back at them.

Both men finished photographing the scene, walked around the area once more and called it quits.

"What a liar," Michael said when they were in the car. "Did he think we wouldn't check on his story?"

Later . . .

When questioned, Bo-Bae refuted Cline's testimony. She said she never heard of and had never been at the Der Schluss place he talked about. She denied knowing anyone named Cisco or Mita and testified to everything she knew of Rick Cline's involvement in kidnapping and human trafficking.

Bo-Bae swore to having been held prisoner at his home for weeks. Her story was corroborated by a neighbor who reported having seen the Asian teenager there. Some of her clothing and personal papers were found at Cline's home and were confiscated.

The police contacted Bo-Bae's family in Seoul, who were overjoyed to learn she was found and she was safe. Her real name, Bo-Bae, meaning 'treasure' or 'precious' in Korean, would be spoken again with happiness.

CHAPTER SIXTEEN

Seventy five thousand gallons of water rushed over the shale and limestone riverbed of the American Falls at Niagara each second, while astonished tourists watched. The roar of its descent was deafening as it tumbled 180 feet downward onto massive piles of debris from the erosion of its base. This section of Niagara Falls was the one that deterred daredevils in barrels from challenging it lest they be crushed on its tonnage. Dainty rainbows and clouds of water shrouded and contrasted the harsh brutality at the basin's seat.

Allen and Vince marveled at the sheer force of the Niagara River tumbling undeterred over the falls. Both men leaned closer over the rail, mesmerized by the beauty and power, neither feeling completely safe despite the barrier between them and the water. A light mist from the water's activity ascended from the falls, spritzing all in its path, moistening the men's hair and clothes.

Vince, in his role as "Daddy," tapped Allen's arm to get his attention and motioned for him to follow. They walked to a picnic table away from the deafening roar, where they could speak without raising their voices. As soon as they reached the setting underneath sheltering trees, a man stepped out from behind them and wordlessly joined them.

Allen made a questioning face and was given an 'ok' sign.

Wands were run up and down their clothing, front to back, side to side. The man frisked both of them and, satisfied with finding nothing of concern, walked away and out of sight.

Vince and Allen sat down opposite each other.

Vince wiped his bald pate and face with a handkerchief, being careful to avoid the scar over his nose.

"What was that?" Allen asked, motioning toward the area where the man who had frisked them had gone.

"Precautions. I told you we'd be checked for bugging devices before we started. We wanted to make sure no one had slipped a device onto either of us. That's important for everyone concerned."

"Oh," Allen said, relieved that nothing was found."It's good seeing you again, Daddy," Allen said. "You've changed since we last met." He motioned to the bald top, with gray hair circling his skull at the base. "You used to have a full head of dark hair. And where did that scar come from?" he asked. "I don't remember that."

"I told you that being an agent was a tough job," Daddy said with a grin. "I've gained a few pounds, too." He patted the uncomfortable padding on his enlarged girth. "Too many phone conferences and not enough exercise."

"You must be feeling pretty good about the success of Bobby's Play," Allen said. He pulled a visor down over a full head of prematurely graying hair to shield his dark eyes. Moisture from the falls glistened on his skin. He wiped his arms and face with a monogrammed handkerchief.

"It was one of our best so far. In that Scene, we were able to satisfy more than one case. The Screenwriters, Cast Members, everyone involved, were superb. I'm proud of them all."

"Not to mention the cost effectiveness of the effort," Allen said. "The Group must have been able to accomplish many of its goals very inexpensively. I didn't get the details of what happened. Can you fill me in on where it was held and who was there?"

"Later, Allen. When I have more time. But you're right. We save a lot of money doing Plays that way. Thanks to the Script and members of the Theater Group giving us the use of their resources, we slashed the bottom line. But, again, that is only one piece of it. Our primary focus remains the provision of justice for our members and their loved ones. We can never forget that, Allen. That is what drives the success of the Theater Group. Loyalty and support is fleeting in other operations, whether it be temporal or ecclesiastical and regardless of purpose or inherent nobility. The Theater Group seeks one thing and one thing only - justice. An Agent must never forget that."

"I understand," Allen said. "After what happened to Barbara, a day hasn't gone by that I don't think about the impact evil has on all of us. She was a talented and beautiful ballerina and now can barely walk. The suffering she has endured has been difficult for all of us who love her." He looked at some tourists walking nearby and stopped speaking. He seemed to be considering weighty matters.

"Are you sure you're ready to take on the responsibilities of being an Agent? I have no doubt you're qualified. I just want to be sure you're prepared emotionally for the load from all you've been through. The pay will be better as an Agent. I know you've incurred a lot of medical bills with Barbara's rehab and can probably use the money."

"I'm ready," Allen said. "As a minority, I can bring another perspective to the operations. Injustice is our daily lot."

"Injustice is everyone's daily lot. It cares not for color or creed," Vince said. "Yet sometimes it is borne of color or creed mostly as an excuse. Globally, it manifests itself when the opportunity permits and when weakness is perceived by those who crave power. Even some minorities may crave power over others. That is a part of life that we must acknowledge. But we don't have to accept injustice as the victor."

Vince changed the subject. "I've brought some more information for you to review. Did you get the files sent to you after we last talked?"

"Yes, I did," Allen said. "That was some heavy reading, but I got through it." He shifted his medium frame to get another view of the falls.

"In the packet I brought for you today, I've outlined the duties that will be yours as the Agent for the West Coast and will discuss them in depth with you," Vince said. "I will remain the Agent for the East Coast. Taking into account population density and land mass, the line of demarcation will be as follows: everything west of and including North Dakota, South Dakota, Nebraska, Kansas, Oklahoma, and Texas will be part of the West Coast Theater Group. I've included Hawaii in your Group and Alaska will stay in the East Coast Group. Once we get you up and running, I'm hoping our recruiters will provide candidates, one each to take over the Alaska and Hawaii Plays. You and I will train them."

Allen listened closely to the presentation, impressed with the depth and scale of the organization. He expressed his admiration for the capabilities of those involved.

"As Solicitor, you reported to me," Vince said. "As the Agent, you will get to know the names and backgrounds of almost all of the members of your Theater Group. Very few of them know any of the other members, though. Once in awhile some of their paths cross if they are in the role of Cast Member. And sometimes they must rehearse and study the Script with others. However, in private life, no acknowledgement is ever given they have seen the other person before. The Theater Group is compartmentalized from their daily life. It is expected of all members. The Scene at the last Play was the largest gathering of Cast Members in one place that we've ever used. Some of them may have recognized others, but they were strict in interacting only with those at their table or booth, unless the Play dictated otherwise. Some of our Patrons who donate money to our cause never participate in any other way with the Group. Occasionally, when needed, one of them will donate their home for use as a Safe House or will assist in another way, but generally, they simply hand over American dollars to the Dollar Dreamers."

"I'm going to miss my role as Solicitor," Allen said. "It was immensely satisfying, finding ways of assisting the Group to negotiate the legal system."

"You were outstanding as a Solicitor," Vince said. "Your position will be hard to fill. Recruiters have been working for awhile now and still haven't found the right person for what has become a full time position. We have to be careful whom we move up into key spots. We have security concerns, you know, and don't want anyone placing our group in danger."

"Thank you," Allen said, shifting uncomfortably. "I will bring the same dedication to my new position as the Agent that I gave as your Solicitor. And you were right about something else that you said. I can use the extra money. Our insurance doesn't cover everything needed for Barbara's care and the bills are mounting. Rehabilitation is expensive."

"I understand. I have confidence you'll do a great job. I have a list here of some new Plays that our Playwrights are working on that will now be your responsibility. The Searchers are doing the background on these and are weeks away from completing their part of the mission. I'll hang onto this information until everything is ready. But, I wanted to discuss them a little with you. You'll get your copies of the Plays when they are finished.

"The first one I wanted to talk about is Lydia's Play. This one is a bit unusual in that the sponsor of the play is not Lydia's husband, family member, or even her boyfriend. He was her childhood sweetheart who still loves her and wants justice. Lydia contracted HIV from a college boyfriend, Phil, who failed to tell her he had tested positive for the disease. Unfortunately, Lydia's immune system was already compromised by another health issue and she died from AIDS last year. Phil denied knowing he was HIV positive when confronted by Lydia, but our sponsor found out he did know it and just didn't tell her. There were three documented witnesses who confirmed Phil knew he had HIV, and we have his medical records to prove it. Our Group requires a double witness so this qualifies for our action. Phil is the Antagonist in this Play. The Theater Group members will continue to report to me on the progress of this and other Plays on the west coast until your group is ready. Then, you will be responsible for putting together the Cast Members and seeing it through to its completion. I'll tell you their real names and the Play's location later.

"The second play is Hazel's Play. After a massive stroke, Hazel was taken off life support by her second husband who claimed that was what she had said she wanted. Her children did not believe him and after her death, found documentation refuting their stepfather's claim. Also a couple of friends informed Hazel's children of their surprise that had happened since Hazel told them she did not want to be taken off, regardless of her condition. Her children are sponsoring this Play.

"The last Play I want you to work on is called September Play. It is sponsored by twenty families of victims of the September 11 attack on our country. Our Group has information on two Al-Qaeda members who had a small part in planning and financing that tragedy. As usual, our first action was to have one of our members try to get justice through the legal system. That is always our first choice of action - give the system a chance to work. Liberal judges and expensive lawyers thwarted the process and it got nowhere. Your Group is getting this Play because the Antagonists now live and work on a compound out west. The Play will be done there.

Again, the real names and locations will be sent to you when we are closer to setting the productions in motion."

"The amount of justice needed for victims is staggering," Allen said. "Practically every day, someone is harmed and the perpetrator goes unpunished."

"True. But we can only take on cases we know meet all our criteria, and we can only proceed with them when the stage is set. Our activities are much different from people who take the law into their own hands. That's why we don't consider ourselves vigilantes. Under no circumstance is the Antagonist murdered. No exceptions. We get them through hard work and perseverance. We pursue justice through the accepted channels like the court system when we can. When the system breaks down and the Antagonist gets away, we move on with the Play. The Searchers role in providing the knowledge base for the play is massive. They are the Group members who obtain background information from families and research about the victim and the guilty party. We do not make a move until everything is in place. That is why we are so successful. We never do half a job. Never. And I will expect the same of you and your Group."

"It's amazing that some of the Antagonists fall for what is dangled in front of them," Allen said.

"There's no end to the size of their egos. And our knowledge of them is the key. We promise the bad guys a lot of what they want and they go for it," Vince said. "We promise their desires. We promise to give it to them now, give it to them cheaply and easily or even free, and tell them it is foolproof. In short, we beat them at their own game."

"Are there ever any problems due to lack of funds?" Allen asked. "I mean, will we always be able to bankroll the Plays we initiate?"

"That's a good question," Vince said. "And the answer is no, there is never a lack of funds. And yes, we will always be able to bankroll what we take on. We have Patrons providing a steady stream of cash. Victims relish funding the justice they believe in for their loved ones. Especially when they know they are getting real value for the dollar. We are good stewards of their money, Allen. I'll go over the records with you to show you." Vince thought for a moment and then said. "There is something else you need to know about the financial end of the Theater Group. Besides Patrons, we have a Backer who is not officially a patron. He is known only to me. I call him the Backer when I speak about him. This Backer oversees our money, and when it gets below a certain point, will fund 100 per cent of what we need. He also plugs any holes we might get into, ensuring our Plays are a success. The Backer is powerful enough to handle anything our Group cannot, pulling strings for anything we need. Anything."

"Who is this Backer?" Allen inquired. "And will I be working directly with him?" *He'd have to be a billionaire. A well-connected billionaire. But which one? There are hundreds and hundreds of billionaires worldwide.*

Vince gave Allen a name. "This name is never to be spoken to anyone else or written down for any reason. The secrecy of his identity is critical to the Group, and we want to make sure we never compromise this man. Understand?"

"Yes," Allen said. "Totally. You can trust me."

"Good. I'm counting on you. Before we take a break, I want to talk to you about one of our Theater Group associates. This man is an intelligent, loyal Group member. He has not forgotten his own personal tragedy that brought him to our Group." Vince said. "This man functions as the permanent driver for each Play. During Charlotte's Play, he was the driver but also one of his jobs was to assure the safety of the Cast. While Charlotte's Play was enacted, he was ready twenty-four/seven to do his part. In his professional life, he had been trained as an Israeli soldier. A member of their elite services, the Shayetet 13. He is valuable for his fidelity and his honor. He understands what it is to fight for survival and knows what it takes to succeed. We have more members of the Group just like him. If anything should ever go wrong with the Play, they are capable of handling it without compromising the ideals and integrity of the Theater Group. Our enemies would not want to be up against these loyal Theater Group members."

Vince stopped talking briefly so Allen would get his point.

"Now, this driver's training is important in taking Cast Members when and where they need to be. And to get them out of a jam, should one arise. He knows what it takes to make things happen and is one of our key associates. I have already alerted the recruiters that we need to find someone with skills equivalent to his, to work with your group. Like the Agent position, this is another critical placement within the Group, and no decision will be made until the right person is found. You can see why it might take awhile to get everything ready for a west coast Group."

"Yes, I see that. Thank you, Daddy," Allen said.

The story of the driver was causing Allen to rethink some things. "I'll wait to hear from the Recruiters about whom they recommend." His countenance was dark as if he suspected a storm was on the cusp.

"Are you ok?"

"Sure. Just tired, that's all," Allen answered, brightening up. "I was just thinking of my wife."

Allen was ruminating over the personal consequences he would suffer if any of those loyal Theater Group members should discover his treachery.

"Speaking of Recruiters, I'll be reassigning two of our own Recruiters to work with you," Vince said. "They will be there to get you up and running and will stay with you for awhile, even after other Recruiters are brought into your Group."

"Great," Allen said, glancing over at the falls again. He needed time to think.

Sensing Allen's need for that break, Vince said, "Let's go take a closer look at the water, have some dinner, and then we'll talk again."

Vince, too, was getting tired from the pressure and long days. His upcoming vacation was looking sweeter and sweeter. "Before we go, is there anything else you want to ask me right now?"

"I've never heard your real name, Daddy. You know mine, but I don't know yours. Will you tell me what it is?" Allen asked.

"I'll reveal that to you when the time is right. I need you to trust me on this one, too." He hoped that everything he had said had made an impact.

"Sure," Allen said.

Together, Allen and the man he knew only as Daddy went back to the railing and watched the plunging waters with the crowd. They exclaimed about the power of the falls, discussed where they were to eat dinner, and in general, looked like two ordinary tourists out having a good time at the great Niagara Falls.

Neither of the men seemed to notice the family snapping photographs of their children who rushed over to stand at the same railing the Agents were leaning against. One snapshot after another was taken, with the subjects of the lenses including, and sometimes exclusively being, Allen and Vince.

Observing the photographic activity were two men wearing sunglasses, with binoculars slung around their necks, partially hidden within a copse of trees.

After Vince retired to his hotel room in the evening, he made some telephone calls.

"Hi, Baby," Vince said. He was feeling burdened by the actions he was forced to take.

"Hi, Vince," Marla said. "You sound tired. How's it going?"

"Good," Vince said. "I was thinking about you and wanted to hear your voice."

"I was thinking about you, too. Is everything okay?" She wished they were together.

"It's going fine. The new Agent is intelligent which helps a lot. There's a steep learning curve to understanding how we operate, but he's doing well. He had a lot of questions about the financial piece which I had to go over with him. I never realized how complicated the Theater Group really is until I had to teach it to him."

"Don't the Dollar Dreamers handle most of the finances?" Marla asked.

"Yes, but I review the records monthly to keep everything secure. That is why anyone who donates to the Group must telephone me and tell me how much they gave."

"No wonder you're tied up all the time," Marla said. "Your job is exhausting."

"Well, there's one aspect of the financial end which I want to share with only you. The Theater Group has a Backer. He also watches the finances, and if we ever need any money at all, the Backer gives it to us out of his personal account."

"Wow," Marla said. "That's wonderful. It must provide you with a great sense of security knowing that."

"Yes, it does," Vince said. Before he hung up the phone, he gave her a name for the Backer.

The next person Vince called was Benjamin. He gave him the same story that he gave Marla and Allen about someone financing the Group whenever needed. Benny was also given a name for the person who was the Theater Group's Backer.

A different Backer name had been given to each of the three whom Vince suspected as being the traitor - Allen, Benny and Marla.

Vince got to sleep later than usual, knowing that the three people who could be the mole now had a name for the Backer. They were the only ones in the Theater Group who had ever seen him in person without a disguise, so they were the only ones who could have given a description of him to the investigators. They were also the only ones who had access to the kind of information the mole had. His heart was heavy, wondering who the traitor was and what he would have to do about it.

It took awhile to get to sleep because of his concerns about people for whom he had love and deep affection. His dreams were haunted by scenes of Allen, Marla, and Benjamin, all turning on the Theater Group and causing it to crumble. Allen, with his ballerina wife, whispering to the authorities that the Theater Group should be burned out; Marla, laughing at him behind his back as she gave their enemies whatever they wanted to know about her lover; Benjamin, turning over secret journals of all his activities as the Driver and personal confidante.

Vince awoke at four am, and, unable to go back to sleep, started his day. Periodically, the potential for Marla being the mole invaded his thoughts, and he shuddered to think his beloved could be the source of such treachery. Mental and physical pain accompanied his entertaining her betrayal.

CHAPTER SEVENTEEN

Much later . . .

Vince situated himself comfortably at his desk, stacks of papers and files fanned out before him. While the day was a good one, he still had nagging doubts about who the mole was. It cast a pall over the happy news that he had for the Theater Group. He pulled some files out which needed his attention, placed them in front of him, and then his thoughts drifted to the Niagara Falls trip and the recent outcome of Bobby's Play.

Today was special for him, Marla, and others. It was special because today Rick Cline was charged with human trafficking, money laundering, assault and battery, attempted rape and possession of child pornography. Cline would finally get what he deserved for brutally raping and injuring Marla's sister Kelly. The Group would monitor the trial and outcome and respond as needed.

This most recent Play, Bobby's Play, became known within the Theater Group as a "Three-Fer." They got three for one money. A trio of families received the justice that had eluded them for a long time. Rick Cline's charges provided satisfaction to Marla and her family and friends. Bobby's Play was also planned and implemented to bring justice to Bo-Bae and her Korean family for her suffering after being kidnapped and forced into sexual slavery by a well-organized international gang. The evidence the Theater Group uncovered and planted on Cline would send many guilty parties to jail for their part in all of that.

The net it cast hauled in some of the lowest criminals who were walking the streets. Those discovered included a foreign diplomat who had immunity from prosecution. Pressure was brought to bear by the right people, one of whom was a Theater Group member, and the diplomat was forced to return to his country of origin. The Theater Group would see to it that he received justice there.

The third family finally getting justice was Ginny Anderson, mother of Bobby Anderson who was murdered by Glen Spade. Bobby's Play culminated in his being charged for drug use and sales. Like most of their Play endings, this one was bittersweet.

Vince picked one of many cell phones out of his desk and punched in the numbers.

"Hi, Daddy," Ginny said. She put down her drink.

"Hi, Ginny. How are you?" Vince asked.

"Better," Ginny said. "My thanks to you and the Cast Members for a job well done. It doesn't bring my son back, but it does bring justice for him and for me. That counts for a lot." She swallowed hard and took another sip of her cocktail.

"Yes. And sometimes, discrete justice is all we can hope for," Vince said. "Still, it is almost as good. We can't always expect the right outcome every time someone is taken to court, given the way some laws and some judges and lawyers protect the criminals. But we can hope to achieve it our way. And, Ginny, we will follow through on the trial, every step of the way."

"I know. Daddy, my investment returns were good this quarter," Ginny said. "I've sent another donation through the Dollar Dreamers. Hopefully, it will help to take more criminals off the street." She told him the amount.

"Thank you," Vince said. "It will be wisely used." He jotted the figure down.

"I know," she said. "That's why I keep giving."

"I hope this will provide you with the peace that you were looking for. Please call me anytime. I always enjoy hearing from you."

"Thank you. Same to you," Ginny said, and vowed that today, she would quit drinking. There will be no need any more to dull the pain. "Goodbye and God bless," Ginny said. She hung up the phone and, for the first time in a long time, gave herself permission to sob out her sorrow for the death of her only child.

Vince took a few minutes to compose himself after speaking with Ginny. While he enjoyed the successful Plays, the responses of the families came with an emotional price for him, too.

He chose a different cell phone and telephoned Bo-Bae's family.

"Hello," a man's voice said in Korean.

"Hello, Sir. This is Daddy calling," Vince said in English

"Hello, Daddy. So good to hear from you," the man said, now speaking perfect English. "It's Daddy," he called to someone in the room with him.

"How is Bo-Bae?" Vince asked. He hadn't heard from her for awhile.

"She is well. Recovering from her ordeal. As her father, I am concerned of course, but she seems to be doing fine. Improving."

"We could not have completed Bobby's Play without her," Vince said. "She was wonderful. And very brave to endure it all. Of course, you know, she was never in any danger. Only Theater Group members were in Der Schluss that night, so if anything had gone wrong, she would have been immediately taken out of there."

"I know that," he said. "It was the ride with Rick Cline that was the worst part. Knowing you had alerted the police and also had Cast Members following them made it easier, but it still was difficult for her and us."

"All I can say is thank you so very much for giving her permission to participate," Vince said. "A vicious criminal was taken off the streets and put where he belongs."

"Yes," he said. "And many of those criminals who take foreign women for their own terrible uses were put away. It was a great victory. Bo-Bae, her mother, and I are forever in your debt, and we owe a huge 'Thank You' to the entire Theater Group."

"You are most welcome, Sir," Vince said. "Before I hang up, I want to thank you for the generous cash you donated to our cause. It was received a couple of weeks ago."

"You are welcome," he said. "It is not the last money you will receive from us. Oh, and Daddy," he said. "I hope to talk to you sometime about starting a Theater Group in my country. Do you think we could meet soon?"

"I'm going on vacation in a week. I'll be away for three weeks but will contact you when I return and we'll discuss it. Thank you, again," Vince said. "And please give our love to your beautiful daughter."

"I will," he said. "I will wait to hear from you. Thank you. Thank you." He went to tell his family that their friend had called.

Again, Vince needed a little time to recover. He thought about the lovely Bo-Bae - the girl they called Angel. She had been rescued from sex slavery by a Theater Group member before Bobby's Play was planned. When the Playwrights were outlining the acts, they skillfully wove three story lines into the one play. Including Bo-Bae's abduction, to get her justice. She was now recovering at her parents' home, attending school, and making plans for her future. After speaking with her father, one of the concerns that nagged Vince about starting a Theater Group chapter in another country was the potential for another mole to try to bring their operation down. Vince also wanted to continue limiting the number of persons who met him face to face. Before proceeding, he would discuss it with the Backer.

Planning the Der Schluss scene took a long time, many Cast Members, and carefully timed execution. The building Der Schluss played out in was owned by Theater Group members, a lovely old couple whose youngest child had been murdered on Nine-Eleven in New York City. Their play, September Play, was coming up in California in the near future. It was to be the most elaborate play the Theater Group attempted, incorporating the resources and cooperation of families of twenty victims of the World Trade Center attack.

Vince smiled as he thought of Der Schluss. The name was chosen because it means 'The End' in German. The playwright chose it, thinking it to be a fitting name for the downfall of murderers, thugs, drug dealers, and those who prey on whomever they can.

Vince relaxed and made his final telephone call for the afternoon. He picked another cell phone from his drawer.

"Hello," a sweet voice said.

"Hello, Baby," Vince said. "I miss you, and I love you." He began to relax.

"Hi, Vince," Marla said. "I miss you, too. And I love you."

"How are your parents doing?" Vince asked. "With Bobby's Play finished, I'm sure they have a reason to smile."

"You better believe it," Marla said. "Even though Kelly doesn't understand what is being said to her, Mom and Dad told her that her attacker will not hurt another woman. And, Vince, Kelly has been weaned from the breathing tube. She is finally breathing on her own. It's a miracle. We are still praying that she will someday regain consciousness and begin her life again."

"That's wonderful news," Vince said. "Kiss her for me, will you?

"I will," Marla said. "I participated in my final Play, Vince. Bobby's Play was the last for me. You know what that means. We are no longer bound by the Theater Group rules and can be together. That makes our upcoming vacation extra special."

"I can hardly wait. Time is almost up, Baby," Vince said. "I have to say goodbye but, before I do, I want to let you know everything is in place for our holiday. I incorporated all of the things you said you wanted to do while we're together. The jet will take us to our vacation spot in exactly one week. Expect the vacation details in a hand delivery from a courier tonight. I love you."

"I love you, too." Marla said.

Vince had not heard yet who the mole was. He was hoping and praying he and Marla would have that vacation and the future he wanted.

CHAPTER EIGHTEEN

"Hi, Vince."

"Hi, Backer," Vince said. "This situation with the mole has been upsetting, but so are a lot of other things we deal with. Let's get on with it. What do you know?"

"The mole has been outed," the Backer said. "We know who it is."

"Tell me everything." Vince said. He held his breath for the answer.

Vince was given the name of the mole, the person who was cooperating with authorities to shut the Theater Group down. He was deeply disappointed but knew he would have felt the same way no matter who the traitor had been.

"The fake Backer whose name you gave to the mole is being investigated by the IRS and the FBI," the Backer said. "The billionaire is under investigation for income tax evasion, illegal campaign contributions and money laundering. They found some suspicious movement of currency from one financial institution to another in his bank accounts. It seems that there are many cryptic layers to the movement of millions of his dollars they believe that he earned through the smuggling of people in and out of Europe, Cuba, Mexico and the United States. Many families of missing children will gain closure from his being investigated, although he's not aware yet that the government is on to him."

"I'm not sorry the billionaire is caught. We were going to do a Play on him for his involvement in illegal activities anyway, and now we won't have to. It spares us the expense and effort. I am sorry though, to hear who the mole is," Vince said. "We'll have to do some damage control real quick. I'll get right on it."

"You'll have to meet with the mole again right away to clean this up. I've already made all of the arrangements for you to go back to Niagara Falls to meet at the same spot you met with Allen.

"Thank you," Vince said. He hung up the phone and telephoned the mole, saying that they needed to meet for business. He explained all questions would be answered when they got to their meeting place. Vince provided the necessary information of where they were to meet and how. He apologized for not being able to send the private jet for transportation to Niagara Falls.

"You'll have to book yourself a flight immediately," Vince said. "Our jet is tied up with transporting Cast Members to a Play that is about to begin. Book it for a one-way flight for your whole family as I'm not sure when we will be finished with our business. Of course, we'll reimburse you," he lied, knowing that this person would never get another cent from the Theater Group he turned against.

"That's okay," the mole said. "I can do that."

"This is one of the downsides of working within the Theater Group, having to drop everything at a moment's notice for business," Vince said. "I'm still not totally used to it. I hope it won't be too difficult for you to get away to attend this meeting. Do you think you can arrange it?"

"Don't worry about it," the mole said. "I'll be able to make arrangements to be there. See you tomorrow." The phone was hung up and another used to make a call to a contact.

"Something new?" A female voice said.

"Yes. I have to meet Daddy tomorrow at Niagara Falls. He has something important he needs to discuss with me. I'm not sure what it is, but it should include more information about the Group. I'll telephone you as soon as I know."

"Great," the female said. "There'll be more photos taken tomorrow because the last ones weren't so good."

"Okay," the mole said. "I better get off of here so I can book a flight."

"Right. We dusted the files you were given for Daddy's fingerprints. So far, nothing's turned up. We're still working on it," she said. "See if you can get him to tell you his real name."

"We should learn much of what we need to know tomorrow," the mole said. "I'm hanging up now because I've got a lot to do."

At Niagara Falls the next day . . .

Leaning against the cluster of trees were the same men who observed the last Niagara Falls meet. They had their sunglasses on and binoculars around their necks. Vince was seated at the picnic table listening to the background sounds of an ancient river tumbling over and downward onto the rocks and riverbed. He blended in with the rest of the visitors, wearing a casual shirt and pants. Everything was planned and timed for the showdown. *This is going to be a tough experience. But one that has to be done.*

A young family was busy trying to take pictures of their children playing near the picnic table where Vince was seated. It was proving to be a difficult task as every time they went to take a photo, a group of college kids playing touch football would run in front of their camera. Frustrated, the photographers, a young man and woman, would watch the ball players moving around, reposition themselves for a good shot, and try again. The large group revised their game strategy each time the person with the camera changed the positioning of their photos.

To a casual observer it looked to be by chance. To the trained eye, it was a game of cat and mouse, designed to minimize capturing Vince on film.

When the mole approached the man he knew as Daddy, the same man was present who had checked for electronic bugging devices at their last meeting. He waved the rod up and down their clothing and frisked them professionally. He was gone as quickly as he had come.

"Good to see you," Vince said to the mole. "I want to tell you again how sorry I am that we weren't able to provide the jet for you. Was your flight comfortable? Is your hotel room okay?"

"Yes, the flight was good," Allen said. "The hotel I booked is nice, too. How about you?"

"Good. Everything is good," Vince said. "I need to make this meeting as short as possible, my wife has gone into labor, and we are expecting our second child soon."

Upon that declaration, the two men who were watching from the trees approached his table.

"We need to leave in a few minutes, sir," one of them said. "I just got word that the baby will be here within the hour." He pointed at his watch.

"Thank you," Vince said. "The reason I wanted to meet with you today, Allen, is we're going to have to postpone starting up the west coast Theater Group. Our Recruiters are having difficulty finding trustworthy staff for your Group. It's taking longer than I thought it would."

Allen started to say something, and Vince put his hand up.

"Please let me finish as I only have a few minutes. Of course, I want you to stay with us as a Solicitor until the west coast Group starts up."

"Of course," Allen said, relieved he was still trusted.

"Sir," one of the men said, pointing again to his watch.

"I'm sorry, Allen, I must go," Vince said. "Babies are on their own schedule." He laughed. "I'll telephone you tomorrow and talk with you at length. And again, please accept my apologies."

"Let me know if it's a boy or a girl, or both," Allen said smiling. He got up to shake the offered hand.

"I will. Stay here awhile and enjoy the sights if you'd like to. The Group will reimburse you for your expenses," he lied.

Unbeknownst to Allen, he would be paying his own way from now on. He would never have another day's work as Solicitor for the Theater Group, nor would Vince speak to him again.

The two men escorted Vince away from the table to a stretch limousine.

When the black car was out of sight, Allen pulled another cell phone from his pocket and told the waiting female the disappointing news.

"Daddy couldn't stay. His wife went into labor, and they are expecting their second child any hour now."

"I'll add that to the profile we have of him," a female voice said. "He has a wife, a child, and one due any time. We know so little about him, so all of this is good. Did he tell you his real name?" She asked.

"No. He was whisked out of here by two associates to attend to his wife. He's going to telephone me tomorrow, so I'll ask him then. We seem to be getting close, so I expect to not have any problem with that. I'll even send him a baby gift once we find out who he really is and where he lives." He laughed nervously, ambivalent about his role as the mole.

"Call me tomorrow as soon as you hear from him," the female said.

"I will," Allen replied and cut off the conversation. He began to think on his conversation with Daddy during their first meeting at Niagara. His focus was Daddy's story of the driver and his loyalty to the Group, a contrast to his own actions. He was getting cold feet and thought that maybe he should have asked Daddy for the money needed for Barbara's care instead of going to the government agency which was trying to bring them down.

While Allen was talking with his contact, Vince, too, was making a phone call.

"How's it going, friend?" Vince asked.

"Great," Benny replied. "Allen's wife and daughter are at Niagara with him so we're able to go through his home, top to bottom. I found all the files you gave him and copies of the pictures his accomplices had taken at your last visit with him at Niagara Falls. You look terrible in these. Nothing like yourself. The makeup artists did a superior job."

"Yeah. Thanks. I think. When I look in the mirror, I don't even recognize myself made up like this. What else is happening there?" Vince asked. He started to pull the fake scar off his nose while talking.

"Everything was well hidden, I've got to give him that," Benny said. "One of our tekkies is cleaning out his computer right now. By the time he's done, it will look like a computer virus wiped the files from his hard drive. Nothing will be retrievable. It will be a great loss for Allen, but he deserves it. It's amazing what our guys can do now," he said admiringly. "Someone is over at Allen's daughter's house right now checking her place out, too. We don't want to miss anything."

"Good," Vince said. "Allen is going to find his whole life has been turned around once he gets home. I've gotta go. Call me when you're finished."

"Okay," Benny said.

Vince peeled the false head covering off his hair and placed it on the seat beside him. He was glad to get the hot thing off. Besides that, he didn't like the way he looked bald with only a halo of hair circling the base of his head. He pulled from under his shirt, the thick padding which made him look fifty pounds heavier than he was. Feeling so much better, he picked up his phone again.

"Hi, Baby," Vince said. "How are you?"

"Almost ready to go," Marla said. "How are you?"

"Just great. Relieved, and just great."

"What do you mean?" Marla asked.

"I'll tell you when we're together. I love you."

"I love you, too."

"I'll telephone you tonight."

"I'll wait to hear from you," Marla answered. She punched the off button on her phone and disposed of it.

CHAPTER NINETEEN

The day before vacation . . .

Packing for the trip was a good experience for Vince. It helped to take his mind off other things. He was almost finished, with only a few items remaining to be picked up before leaving the next day.

The Theater Group Plays were all completed for now, and future ones were on schedule to begin in five weeks. Vince felt comfortable delegating responsibility for overseeing the projects to Benny.

He retrieved a cell phone and punched in some numbers.

"Hi, Backer, how are you?" Vince asked.

"Good. Ready for your three weeks of nothing but fun and frolic?"

"You bet," Vince said. "I have some business questions first. Have your heard anything about what has happened to Allen? I'm not concerned about that no good turncoat, but I am concerned about how all of this is going to affect his wife. She's not a well woman."

"It's all taken care of. Allen has been recruited by a corporation to do some work for them in Paris. How about that? He took the offer since the task force that was investigating the Theater Group was disbanded. Nothing Allen gave them had any real value, and pressure came from somewhere higher up to pull the plug on the investigation. A gag order has been placed on anything connected to the Theater Group, and Allen has been ordered to keep quiet about it or risk losing his new position. All of the leads he provided went nowhere. Your fingerprints were a dead end. By the way, those photos of you they took at Niagara were horrible. Makes me wonder what any woman would see in you."

"Hey, I think the makeup artists did a great job on me for those pictures," Vince said, laughing.

"They sure did. You were one homely looking Agent," the Backer said.

"What about Allen's family? Will they be all right?"

"Yes, they'll be fine. Barbara and their daughter will be traveling with him to Paris. Their daughter has transferred to a university there. He's lucky that we care so much about his family. If it would have been just him, he'd have been sent to some desert country to work. Somewhere hot and barren. Or maybe somewhere just the opposite with lots of minus degrees. Like the South Pole. He deserved to go somewhere punishing after what he tried to do to the Theater Group. Allen is promised a good salary for his new position and should be all right as long as he keeps his mouth shut. He knows the problems that could find him should he mention anything about the Theater Group ever again. We shall see. He's being watched, and he's aware of it."

"Thanks for letting me know," Vince said. "I've been thinking about his wife and hoping she didn't have to suffer further. I'm glad she'll be okay through all of this."

"You're a good man," the Backer said. "Not everyone would have been so concerned about an enemy's family."

"I've received a new request for a Play and want you to take a look at it," Vince said. "It's from a family whose daughter was murdered by one of the guns from the "Fast and Furious" gunrunning debacle. There's plenty of documented evidence of that being the cause, both from witnesses and government papers. The cover up that was attempted is astonishing. Once you look it over and think we should move forward, I'll start making plans for it."

"Send it to me today," the Backer said. "I'll have Benny look at it with me, and we'll let you know what we think. If it's credible, I know exactly whom to contact in Washington about it. Now, get off the phone and finish getting ready for your vacation. I'll talk to you soon."

CHAPTER TWENTY

Moored off the coast of Italy, the multi-tiered super-yacht, The Morning Star, lazily sloshed in the most beautiful waters that Marla had ever seen. She beheld blue seascape almost brighter and bluer than the brain can process - bluer and more beautiful than man could ever create. She adjusted her sunglasses to protect her eyes from the brilliance of the incandescent waves undulating across the Tyrrhenian Sea toward the beaches of the coastal Lazio region, her Italian destination of choice.

"Hi, Baby," Vince said, holding a glass of freshly squeezed lemonade out for her to take. "I have something for you." He sat down next to her, watching her every move.

Marla rolled over onto her back on the lounge chair, adjusted her bikini, and waved up at her lover. The tip of an Atala butterfly tattoo was visible above the skimpy bikini bottom. Marla retrieved the juice, took a sip, and let out a sigh. She closed her eyes to enjoy it, then opened them again. She felt like she was in Paradise.

"Come to join me?" She put the glass of lemonade on a stand.

"Uh huh," Vince said, bending over to kiss her.

They embraced gently, enjoying the tender kiss of a couple in love.

Vince whispered how much he loved her.

Marla returned the sentiments and thanked him for orchestrating the most beautiful vacation she had ever had. She gently touched his now-short dark hair.

"I had to cut my hair so I could wear the bald piece for the Niagara Falls meeting," Vince said. "I kinda like it this way." He brushed his hands back over the close crop.

"You look so handsome," Marla said.

Vince seated himself in a deck chair next to her lounger. "Need me to rub some suntan lotion on you?" he asked hopefully.

"Anytime," Marla said, rolling onto her stomach.

Vince butterflied the lotion across her body.

She rolled over so he could lotion her stomach.

Vince willingly obliged. He was gentle, making sure to cover every inch of exposed flesh so her pale skin would be protected from the sun's damaging rays.

"We'll be situated off the coast of Rome tomorrow," Vince said. "We were granted permission to enter Vatican City, where we will have an audience with the Pope. I know how much you wanted to go there. It was number one on your list, right above the thermal spas of Emilia-Romagna and the Egyptian Museum in Turin. We'll be doing everything you wanted, Baby." He got as much pleasure from telling her as she did from hearing it. Since eliminating her from his list as the mole, Vince felt closer to her than ever.

"How did you ever manage all this?" Marla said. "A three-week cruise on a 450-foot yacht, stops wherever we want, and an audience with the Pope! What King of the World do you know?" While she was kidding, she really wondered how he had arranged such seemingly impossible requests. Much of what they were going to do required a lot of resources and a powerful person to make it happen.

"The Morning Star's owner made the arrangements," Vince said. "He knows someone who knows someone who knows the Pope." Vince laughed. "Actually, he knows everyone who is anyone who knows anyone."

"Who is the owner?" Marla asked. "You never told me who this magnificent ship belongs to."

Since boarding at the start of their vacation, she still hadn't adjusted to its size and grandeur. Everything anyone could want was on board, with all of their needs met by a caring, although unobtrusive crew.

"The owner wishes to remain anonymous for now. I can tell you that he is the real benefactor of the Theater Group. He provided this vacation to us as a thank you for all we do to arrange and facilitate

Plays. I call him the Backer. He is the man behind the name I gave to you recently. Marla, that name was not his real name. It was just a cover. Our Group survives not only due to our own hard work but also because of him. He's the one who started the Theater Group."

"When our vacation is over, I'll write him a thank you note. Will you give it to him for me?" Marla asked. "He deserves it. And more."

"I will," Vince said. "He will appreciate that. Who knows. Maybe you'll get to give it to him yourself. A lot could happen in the three weeks we're together."

"I'd love that. Now, on a different topic. You know why I want to go to The Vatican, don't you?" Marla said.

She wanted to share this part of her beliefs and life with the man she loved. Along with her love for him, her love of family was important, and her request to see the Pope was tied to them.

"I have an idea," Vince said. "You want him to pray for your sister, Kelly. You will be Kelly's proxy when he lays hands on you and petitions God for a miracle. Am I right?"

"You are right," Marla said, amazed at his insight. "I have so much, and she is missing out on life. I want to do that for her. You didn't know her before she was attacked. She was so beautiful and sweet. She had a lot of spunk, and everyone who met her, liked her. She was a great sister, too. We're best friends." She became quiet for a moment "Do you think I'm foolish for making that request?"

"Not at all. I think you are unselfish. And a wonderful sister. And beautiful. And," before Vince could continue, the ship's whistle began blaring.

He immediately became alarmed. "Don't move, Marla."

Upset by Vince's order, she looked around at the half dozen bodyguards who seemingly appeared out of nowhere. Their weapons were drawn, and their eyes were focused on something out on the ocean.

"Who are these people, Vince?"

"I'll explain later. Just do what they say." He hugged her close and moved her toward two of the men for protection.

"What's going on, Carlo?" Vince asked the group's leader.

Carlo pointed to the water. "We're being approached by another boat. It's getting too close, and we don't like it. The name on the side is 'The Sabre.' We pulled it up on our computer, and it's a stolen fishing vessel. Some pirates got it a couple weeks ago. Everyone's been trying to find the boat and the crew who were kidnapped when the boat was hijacked. This doesn't look good."

Carlo barked orders for the two men with Marla to escort her to the ship's safe room.

"Vince," Marla screamed. She broke loose and ran to him.

"Don't worry, darling. You'll be ok. You can trust these men." He wrapped a beach towel around her, kissed her, and motioned for them to escort her away. "Take good care of her."

They nodded.

Carlo tossed a protective vest to Vince and handed him an AK-47. "Hold tight. Put the vest on, stand back, and let us do our jobs. Use the gun if you have to."

Vince donned the vest, clung to the weapon and did as he was told.

The fishing vessel maneuvered closer to The Morning Star.

Through binoculars, Carlo searched amongst the vessel's crew. He shouted to his men. "I see 12 of them. Most look young. They have rocket launchers and AK-47's. Lots of ammo."

Grappling hooks and rope littered the deck of the The Sabre, and the rag-tag gang brazenly stood in the open, weapons ready. A flag crept up the flagpole; skull and crossbones and crossed swords outlined in black and white were waving in the wind.

"I think these clowns want a hijacking," Carlo said, amazed. "I guess they don't know who they're dealing with."

"Who are they dealing with?" Vince shouted, knowing full well what their reply would be.

"Heaven's Door," Carlo and his men shouted back, referring to the name they called themselves to show their determination to win or die trying.

One of the dirty, young pirates made his declaration in return, through an electronic megaphone. "We're coming aboard. Don't try to resist or you'll regret it."

"They have electronic megaphones, GPS systems, and rocket launchers," Carlo said. "But they don't have what we have."

Two of the pirates grasped grappling hooks and made ready to toss them onto The Morning Star's rail. Rounds of bullets from their crew raked the super-yacht's hull. Smoke covered their vessel, and the stench of powder was strong. The pirates focused their weapons in anticipation of the bigger vessel's cooperation.

The ship's whistle sounded again, this time longer and more urgent.

Carlo barked back through his megaphone, "You have one chance and one chance only. Get away from our ship, or you will be the ones regretting it."

Several of the pirates started laughing and poking each other. Their leader responded. "We want your ship and everything on it. And we're not leaving here without it."

"You're not getting a thing," Carlo yelled back. "Now get moving or face the consequences."

"What is going on here?" Vince asked. "What do they want?"

"They want a ransom. Probably millions of dollars. And they want the ship and everything on it." Carlo said. "These uneducated low-life's get paid very little for risking their lives to hijack ships and their crews. They give all that money and everything they steal, to their bosses. Whoever they are."

"We're coming aboard," the pirate leader said. "And you can't stop us."

"Not gonna happen," Carlo answered. "Who are you working for?"

The pirates laughed some more and answered, "Stop talking and give up. We're coming aboard." Bullets whizzed across the ship's deck from the pirates' weapons. Some of the stronger, younger ones readied grappling hooks for tossing onto the ship's rail.

"Put these on," Carlo said, tossing hearing protective headgear to Vince. He and the bodyguards donned theirs and stood their ground. "Get ready everyone."

From somewhere on one of The Morning Star's upper decks, weapons fired and the pirate flag was destroyed. Bits of the smoking, tattered cloth floated into the ocean. After more rounds were let loose, the mast of The Sabre was shot into pieces, cracking and splintering to the shattered deck below.

The pirates stared in disbelief. Two of them had assault weapons shot from their grips. Clutching hands and arms in pain, they tried to find protection. Their guns were retrieved by fellow pirates who positioned themselves to shoot back. Yelling and cursing, they ducked behind boxes and debris, tossing things about and readying for battle.

Before they had a chance to return fire for the boat damage and shootings of their men, a burst of painful ear-piercing sounds emitted from a Long Range Acoustic Device located on the super-yacht.

The unprepared pirates screamed and attempted to protect their ears by covering them with their hands. Some of the men fell to the ground, writhing around. Those who could do so, went below deck.

When the sound ceased, Carlo used the LRAD speaker, clearly warning the pirates, "Get out of here now, or we will sink your vessel and all of you will go down with it."

Another short burst of painful LRAD sounds followed the command.

Shouting and scrambling on deck, the pirates scattered for what meager cover the damaged fishing vessel offered to get away from the debilitating sound.

"Who are you working for?" Carlo yelled again.

The pirates refused to reply and, their boat taking on water, The Sabre began to limp away from The Morning Star. Before long, the stolen craft was just a dot on the horizon.

"Good job men," Vince said, congratulating Carlo and the team.

"Thank you. This is what we plan for," Carlo said. "And a special thank you to the developers of the LRAD and to you for purchasing it. After the USS Cole was attacked in 2000, that weapon was designed, and we're proud to have it for our own use."

"What's our next step?" Vince asked.

"We'll report this incident to the Piracy Reporting Centre so they can warn other vessels in the area and try to retrieve The Sabre for its rightful owners. If the pirates return, we will sink them and their ship without warning, according to our policy."

Vince and Carlo informed the Backer about what had taken place with the pirates.

"I'll be in touch with my friends in Washington, and we'll get to the bottom of this," the Backer said.

Later . . .

Back on deck, Vince and Marla were once again lounging and trying to relax from the piracy ordeal. Vince held her close, comforting her and explaining what had happened. He omitted the part where the pirates planned on confiscating everything and kidnap everyone on board.

"Now where were we before we were interrupted earlier?" Vince said. "Oh yes. I remember now. I was saying how unselfish you were, and I was just about to ask you to marry me."

Marla sat up, facing him. "Say that again." She placed her hands on his arms and leaned toward him so as not to miss a word.

Teasingly, Vince said, "I think you're unselfish, and."

"Not that part," Marla interrupted. "The 'will you marry me' part."

Vince dropped down onto one knee, pulled a silver ring case out of his pocket and looked into her beautiful gold-colored eyes.

"I said I want you to marry me. I already asked your father for your hand in marriage, and he said 'yes.' Will you say 'yes,' Marla? Will you marry me?" He opened the ring case.

"Yes, I will marry you," she said, her eyes misting over. Then she added softly, "You already asked my Dad?" What other surprises could this man have for her?

"Yes, I did," Vince said. "I stopped by to see your parents on my way back from Niagara Falls. Your father and mother graciously agreed that I could propose to you. They are lovely people. I see where you get your sweet personality from. I stopped in to see Kelly, too, and told her all about us. Even if she may not understand, I wanted to tell her."

"Thank you. That was so sweet of you to visit her."

Vince took the diamond ring out of the box and placed it on the third finger of her left hand. The diamond flickered in its setting as it picked up the bright sea light.

"Perfect fit," he said. He pulled her close and held her tight. He kissed her hair, her neck and her lips. "Marla, you mean so much to me, in a way you may not realize. I have always felt safe and loved by my parents, even after I was kidnapped as a child. They did everything possible to find me and deal with those responsible. I fell in love with you the first night I met you and you spoke about your sister Kelly, how much you love her, and how you joined the Theater Group just to get justice for her and for others who have been wronged. You did all that, regardless of the cost to you and the danger you were in. I love that about you. You are not only beautiful and smart but you make me feel safe and loved as no other woman has. I know you would do for me as you did for Kelly, and you know I would do the same for you, too. We are soul-mates, Marla; meant to be together. Two people who have the same love and devotion to one another and to family. Two people in love who will always be there for each other. No matter what. I am thankful to have you in my life."

Tears streamed down Marla's cheeks, and she hugged Vince tightly.

"Congratulations to both of you," Jose, one of the Filipino stewards said. "I apologize for interrupting this special moment. Please, let me take some pictures of the two of you celebrating your engagement. My boss insists."

The couple posed, and Jose took several photos. He took snapshots of them standing, sitting, holding the ring out, and close-ups of the couple smiling at each other. "I will have the prints on your pillow tonight," he said to Marla. "Copies will be e-mailed to the boss and his wife."

"Thank you, Jose," Marla said. "I really appreciate that." She held up the engagement ring for him to see.

"It's beautiful," Jose said. "I know you two will be very happy." Then, in a more serious tone, he said, "May I have a word with you, Mr. Warren?"

"Certainly," Vince said.

"I'll be right back," he said to Marla.

"Please excuse us," Jose said to the newly engaged woman. He bowed politely.

She nodded her head and then stared at her ring. She couldn't stop looking at it.

Jose and Vince walked briskly down a flight of steps and into the steward's private quarters. They crossed the floor to the communications station.

"My boss wishes to have a few words with you." He handed Vince a cell phone. "It will ring in three minutes. I'll go up and tell Marla you will return shortly." Jose bowed and closed the door behind him, leaving Vince alone to wait for the call.

The cell phone rang in exactly three minutes.

"Vince," a strong male voice said. "Did she say yes?" The Backer was eager to hear the news.

"She did," Vince said.

"Your mother and I are so happy for you."

"Vince, darling, I am thrilled to hear your news," his mother said into the phone.

"Thank you, Mom and Dad," Vince said. "And thank you for the vacation. We are having a wonderful time."

"You are most welcome, son," his father said. "When will you tell Marla who I am? Now that you two are engaged, your mother and I want to meet her. She needs to know all about us since you are going to marry her and bring her into our family."

"I will tell her about you this evening. I just wanted Marla to accept a proposal from me without her knowing who you are. I needed to be sure she was marrying me for me. Not because of who my parents are. I've waited a long time for someone like her. I was beginning to think it might not happen."

"I understand, Vince."

His mother said. "Congratulations. I couldn't be happier for you. I can't wait to meet Marla. We want to see both of you soon. I saw the photograph that you sent of her. She's beautiful. I am so excited you are engaged."

"I was thinking that maybe you and Dad could meet up with us in Rome tomorrow. After our visit at the Vatican. How does that sound?"

"It will have to be for dinner. About 8 pm," his father said. "I'm meeting with the Italian Prime Minister earlier in the day. I'll clear my schedule for the rest of the evening."

"Perfect. Will you join us here on the yacht or somewhere in Rome?"

"I'll call you tomorrow and let you know," his mother said. "I love you."

"I love you too, Mom," Vince said. "And Dad, you're still my favorite Backer," he said laughing.

"And you're still my favorite son," his father said.

"But I'm your only son," Vince said.

"Yeah," his father said. "But you don't have to be my favorite, and you are."

The two laughed at this ritual banter that they did about their only child Vince being their favorite.

"I'll see you tomorrow," his father said. "We can hardly wait to meet our new family member."

After hanging up the telephone, Vince's father turned to his wife and said, "Emma, I remember so well how we got started in this Theater Group."

Emma's face became stern. "I'll never forget it, darling. Those days right before you started the Theater Group were the worst days of our lives. I thank God every day for the way it turned out."

She thought about how they almost lost their son when he was kidnapped by a terrorist group which held him for an enormous ransom. For a few days, they didn't know if he was dead or alive.

"If it hadn't been for the Searchers we sent to look for him, we would have never known for sure who was behind it or where they were," her husband said. "We knew Vince was being held by terrorists who were in it for the money they could get to help finance their cause, but we would never have been sure exactly which persons were directly involved. The people we hired saved our son's life, and that singular event provided the impetus for our wanting to get justice. I will protect the Theater Group with everything I have at my disposal."

"I'm behind you all the way, darling. The authorities did everything they could, and it was their behind the scenes negotiating that brought our son back alive," Emma said. "But they were never able to capture the men responsible. As his mother, I wanted justice for what they put our family through. So help me, I could have pulled the trigger myself on each one of them who put our son's life in danger. But thanks to the Theater Group you put together, we got our justice in a different way. And the terrorists' political backers never knew what hit them. It was the Theater Group's first Play."

"And we got the ransom money back, too," her husband said. "They can rot in that third-world prison where they are now, for all I care."

"Let's not talk about it anymore," Emma said. "It only upsets us." She leaned her silvery gray head on his shoulder. Her husband put his arms around her and they held each other tightly.

Later in the evening . . .

The yellow lights glimmered along the darkened coast of Italy as if in competition with the star-filled cloudless sky. The Morning Star was slowly moving north toward Rome. Marla and Vince were enjoying dinner on the top deck with the twinkling space their canopy.

"How will we get from the yacht to The Vatican?" Marla asked. The candlelight shimmered across her face, making her even more beautiful than ever. The diamond engagement ring danced bursts of color upon her hand.

"The Morning Star has a helipad," Vince said. "We will be flown to The Vatican in the owner's helicopter. There is also a hangar for small aircraft if we wish to use one of those."

"This yacht has everything," Marla said admiringly.

"I really need to take you on a complete tour of it soon. But let me tell you about what we are vacationing on," Vince said. "It has its own submarine, gym, spa, screening room, swimming pool, ballroom, etcetera, etcetera, etcetera. It is fully staffed and stocked and exclusively ours for three full weeks."

He smiled and raised his champagne flute in a toast. "To us," he said.

"To us," Marla said.

The engaged couple leaned in toward the table, wrapped their right arm around the other's arm, and drank from the crystal stemware. Violin music strayed faintly into their private bliss as they lowered their glasses for lips to meet lips.

"Now, there's something I must tell you about me and the owners of The Morning Star," Vince said.

Back in Washington, D.C. in a restaurant . . .

"I'm sorry to say this, but we must start from scratch, Nelson. Allen as a mole proved to be a bust. What a waste. The only data he gave us of any value was a listing of two of the Theater Group's committees. We know about the Recruiters and the Solicitors, all about them, but we still don't know who they are, who the Agent is, and, most importantly, who the Backer is," the Chairman said. "Even the description Allen originally gave us of the Agent doesn't match his Niagara picture at all. The others who saw him there said he looked older and heavier than Allen first reported."

The Chairman was disgusted and threw a folder onto his desk. "The only member of the Theater Group we know for sure is Allen. And he's not with them anymore. Got some cushy job in Paris. Took his family, sold his home and moved overseas. After all the money we deposited in his account for his testimony, he flies the coop. And with everyone's blessing." The Chairman leaned back in his chair. "What is your take on all this?"

"We lost a large sum trying to find out who this Theater Group really is," Nelson, the other task force member said. "Allen told us why they do it, but he didn't know any of the other people involved. He didn't know anything for sure except that there are Recruiters and Solicitors. According to him, he wasn't able to learn anything else. The information the Agent gave him was skimpy, sterile, and nothing that we didn't already know. Before he left the country, Allen testified that he knew absolutely nothing else. He clammed up." Nelson took a long drink of his draft.

"The Agent and the Backer must have known we were on to them and that Allen was the mole. They must have," the Chairman said. "If the Agent would have trusted Allen, he would have given him a lot more than he did. It's either that or Allen was stringing us along the whole time. And I don't want to believe that. I'm not even going to offer that as an excuse. After all the time and money bankrolled for this investigation, our heads would roll if anyone suspected Allen was a double-agent."

"What I want to know is who cleaned out Allen's home?" Nelson said. "When he and his family returned from Niagara Falls, all the Theater Group information was gone. Everything. Allen's personal and professional computer files, both the hard copies and the documentation on his computer, were gone. We don't know how that could have happened. The timing was too good for it to be a coincidence."

"It had to be the Theater Group," the Chairman said. "I don't know anyone else who would have benefited from that. Do you?"

"No, I don't. But Allen's neighbors didn't see any vehicles at their home and no suspicious activity. No one can pull off something like that without someone seeing them. I don't care what anyone says. There's usually some clue left behind. Some trace that someone was in that home. But there was nothing. I don't get it. Who are we up against here?" Nelson said. "Nobody has that much power at their disposal." He was disgusted. He was also worried about who their adversary was. If the Agent and Backer could accomplish all that, what else could they do to this investigation? What could they do to him personally?

"The only thing I learned for sure is that the Backer is a female. What worries me the most is she was able to get the original task force disbanded. It's not even to be talked about within the agency. And she and her supporters got Allen that position in Paris. I just know it. I want her," the Chairman said, slamming his fist on the table.

"I'll stay with it as long as you want me," Nelson said.

"It's possible that there is someone other than the Theater Group that somehow is involved here," the Chairman said. "Now that I think about it, maybe the Agent and the Backer aren't the ones who sabotaged everything. We're in Washington, D.C. Anything goes here."

"True," Nelson said, entertaining the thought of a third player in the mix. "I'm just surprised you're willing to entertain that possibility."

"I know how this town works. There may be connections but no one can be trusted. Everyone has an agenda, and they'll throw you under the bus first chance they get to save their own necks or cause. We've got to look at every possible scenario. It's up to us, Nelson. You and I are the only persons allowed to work this secret task force. We answer directly to the Vice President. Do you understand? There's to be no discussion of this with anyone. It's not even Top Secret. It's way above that."

"I understand," Nelson said. "Where do we start?" He hadn't a clue what to do or when to do it. It seemed like a daunting task, and he was in way over his head.

"How many billionaires are there?" the Chairman asked. "Don't tell me. I'll tell you. Several hundred all over the world. And the number goes up every day. We've got a big job ahead of us. Every one of them is going to be scrutinized. By the time we're done with this, there won't be a secret in any of their lives we haven't heard."

"How much can the two of us do?" Nelson asked. "We'll need some outside help. This job is too big for just you and me. We're good, but we're not that good." He was beginning to obsess about the enormity of their mission. Two guys in a small office in D.C. couldn't possibly complete this task alone.

"You had better be that good, because I hand-picked you. I told them you were the best. And the fate of this task force and its outcome is in our hands. We can't let the Theater Group continue to operate like they have. It would cause a lot of law enforcement issues if word of their Group's activities gets into the wrong hands and publicized. Court cases would be thrown out all over this country if this got out. I can just see it. Defense attorneys would claim that any aberration in their case was due to the Theater Group. Judges and lawyers would be tripping all over themselves doing damage control. They'd be nullifying trial outcomes, throwing out evidence, canceling criminal sentences, releasing the prisoners and suing everyone and anyone. It could unseat the President if the opposing party finds out that the Theater Group was able to circumvent the legal system and squash any threats to its agenda. It's not going to be easy, and it's not going to happen tomorrow, but somehow, someday, we'll break the Theater Group."

"I must be frank with you," Nelson said. "I know you think I'm the best, but I don't even know what direction to go with this now."

"I'll be leading the way," the Chairman said. "You'll get your assignments from me. Most importantly, we can only trust each other."

"I'm ready to continue," Nelson said. "And thank you for believing in me that I can handle something this sensitive and important." Feeling overwhelmed and under-equipped, and knowing his below-average past job performance, he questioned his place in the investigation.

"You're welcome," the Chairman said. "We'll start tomorrow. See you in my office first thing in the morning."

During his ride home, Nelson took stock of what the job meant to him. *I like the pay. It's good. But I don't really care one bit if we find the Theater Group's Agent and Backer or not. I'll just follow the leader and do what I'm told. Who knows? This could take a long, long time. Maybe even until I retire.* He was beginning to warm up to what was ahead.

When Nelson was out of sight, the Chairman checked in with the Backer.

"Hey. How are you? How's the new Task Force coming along?" The Backer asked.

"Good. It's now just Nelson and me. Nelson's not the best. Not even close. But I hand-picked him to be the last member involved with the committee because of that. He's mine for the duration. And I report directly to the Vice President. Officially, we start anew tomorrow. By the way, Nelson thinks you're a woman. I just thought I'd throw that in to add one more problem for the investigation."

"I appreciate all you do for the Theater Group. Since we did the Play for your granddaughter, you've been such a big help to us."

"I can't thank the Group enough for what they did. Shelly was avenged, and we are grateful for it. It gave her grandmother and me some peace and comfort. Oh, by the way, I have the information you wanted from the pirates who hijacked The Sabre. The Coast Guard intercepted them just before their vessel sank and managed to save them. The younger ones were thrilled to tell us everything we wanted to know after we made them an offer that was very much to their liking."

"I look forward to reading your report. Did you find out who was bankrolling them?" the Backer asked.

"Yes, and you will be surprised to see who it was. This goes all the way to the top in more than one country."

"What will happen to the pirates who gave you the information?"

"Let's just say they will be joining a group of Ex-Gitmo Uighurs at their government-sponsored island home."

"Excellent." the Backer said. "Let me know when you finally disband your Committee and Nelson gets reassigned somewhere else."

"You will hear from me regularly."

"One last thing," the Backer said. "I'm eager to receive the rest of the information on the Fast and Furious gunrunning fiasco. I'm counting on you."

EPILOGUE

"Hi Daddy, how are you doing?" John Patel said. "Good to hear from you."

"Good, John, how about you?" the Agent said.

"I have good news for you. As you know, Karl Blass has been found guilty of first degree murder in the death of Lissa Powell. The judge has decided to take the jurors' recommendation for sentencing, and Blass has been given the death penalty. Charlotte's Play is finally over."

"That is very good news," Daddy said. "And I hear from one of my other sources that Blass is to be extradited up and down the east coast to face trial for other murders. Hopefully, those victims' families will get their day in court before Blass is executed."

"Great," John said. "I feel almost as good as I did when we did Suri's Play."

"I've thought about your daughter often, John. Such a beautiful little girl. Her story really touched me."

He observed Suri's photo on the wall, in its place amongst the many others for whom a play was executed. The little girl's picture joined those in row after row of victims who had been denied their justice in court, but for whom a Play had gained what they were denied through legal channels.

"Her killer won't be doing that again, thank God, and thanks to The Theater Group," John said. "My daughter was struck down by a cowardly hit-and-run driver who fled and left her on the side of the road to die. He's serving a well-deserved life sentence." John's grief was still palpable even though he felt a measure of relief.

"Has one of our Group been keeping you informed about how that's going?"

"I get a call whenever there's anything significant to report," John said. "Thank you for making that happen."

"It's standard procedure for our group, John. The victim's family gets regular reports after the Antagonist is convicted and his sentence is carried out. I'm only sorry he didn't get the death penalty. But he won't be running anyone else down for a long, long time, if ever."

"This is almost as good," John said.

"I appreciate your giving us the update on Blass," Daddy said. "Take care of yourself, and I hope to talk to you soon. Call me when Blass' sentence is carried out."

"One thing, Daddy," John said. "The police are trying really hard to find out who forged Lissa's identification papers and also who leaked the story to the press about Blass' past lie detector tests. Will there be some trouble from this?"

"I don't think so," Daddy said, "But I'll check it out and let you know."

Daddy turned off his cell phone and picked another one out of the desk to make his next call.

"Marvin, how are you doing?" Daddy said when the Searcher answered the phone.

"Great, Daddy," Marvin said. "What can I do for you?"

"Double-check for me which one of the Players tipped the papers off to the Blass lie detector story. I want to make sure it's secure. The police are putting in time trying to find out who did Lissa's ID paperwork and who tipped the papers off to the Blass story. Since one of our Solicitors did the paperwork, I'm not worried about that. They'll never figure it out. But I am concerned about the tip-off."

"I'll check on it right away, and I'll call you back as soon as I know anything," Marvin said.

"Thanks, I'll be waiting to hear from you." Vince set the phone next to some work he was doing while he waited to hear back from the Searcher.

Vince's Agent's duties continued to be plentiful. He was hand-delivered the script for each Play, oversaw the Theater Group finances, received and handled all the calls from the cast members during the execution of the Play, knew all the participants in each Play, and sometimes explained the rules of the group to new recruits. Despite his handling the production, there were often minutiae of which he wasn't always aware. This was one of those times, and Daddy was interested in how the newspaper tip-off was accomplished.

The Dollar Dreamers had submitted their latest report on their finances to him. He scrutinized the records and was pleased with the results. All of the expenses for Charlotte's Play had been paid, and their cash balance was higher than ever. Patrons had been donating regularly, some with amounts of five and six figures. Except for arranging transportation and accommodations for new recruits, Daddy hadn't needed to call on their Backer for bailout money in a long time.

One philanthropist gave a seven-figure donation after his pet dogs were poisoned to death by a jilted lover. The Doggie Play went off without a hitch after the celebrity girlfriend was located. She was brought up on charges, and her name dragged through the mud on tabloids and television.

She remained unrepentant.

"He and his filthy dogs had it coming to them," was her reply to the numerous paparazzi who had followed her around, taking photos and publishing them.

While her sentence wasn't as severe as her ex would have liked, he was finding other ways to make her pay for what she had done to his beloved pets. Thanks to him, she would never work in her profession again. As an additional "Thank You" to the Group, he gave another large donation to them after her conviction for animal cruelty.

One of Daddy's phones rang and he answered.

"Hi, Daddy," Marvin said. "I have the information you wanted."

"Great. What do you know?"

"The leak to the press for the story about Blass beating the lie detector tests came from within the news community itself. One of their employees is a Cast member and she brought forth the story after learning about the lawyer giving him a new lie detector test he passed. The beauty of the leak is, it was in the papers the same day, and side-by-side with an article about his beating the polygraph done for his defense."

"Is she covered?" Daddy asked.

"In many layers," Marvin said. "They may someday find out it was her, but she'll claim that she happened on her story while doing research on the case. It's plausible and solid."

"Good," Daddy said. With all of his duties and the emotional toll they took, at the end of the day, Vince was pleased he and Marla had married and he would be going home to her.

Holly Fox Vellekoop

ABOUT THE AUTHOR

Holly Fox Vellekoop, MSN, worked for many years as a registered nurse at a state mental hospital. She retired as a Clinical Instructor in Psychiatric and Mental Health Nursing for Penn State University. Holly has a murder mystery, *"STONE HAVEN: Murder Along the River,"* published by Avalon Books, a division of Thomas Bouregy Publishing of New York and has also had newspaper and magazine articles and poems published. She is also the author *of "How to Help When Parents Grieve: Practical Methods to Help Grieving Parents."* She currently lives in Florida with her husband, Dr. Ronald Vellekoop.

Visit the author at www.hollyfoxvellekoop.com.

Made in the USA
Charleston, SC
09 April 2012